TAKE A PLANET.

Take it when you are one hundred strong (or rather weak and weary), and are twenty empty years out from Man's native and only previous home. Take it when your great sub-light ship is wearing out its systems, and you can neither return nor voyage onward; and when, unaccountably, your radio pointed at Sol emits only eternal silence.

Then let your planet teem with life, but no rational beings. Let it welcome you, warm from pole to pole like that Tertiary Earth, innocent of ice or man, that we have all lost. Let it be in some ways a more earthly Earth, with the stars but dimly and seldom visible from its surface; its years, mass, and atmosphere like those of lost Earth, only a little more of each. Let your landers put down on the shore of its one great continent, and your people step gladly out on its blue grass, and walk among its purple trees and harmless beasts, and breathe the bittersweet air of that Eden, that New Earth.

Let some of them kneel, and give thanks to their invisible Lord.

And then let them all taste of the new fruits, the new fishes, the new meats—and find every form of living tissue totally and forever inedible, useless, irrelevant. . . .

G. Barr

THE RIGHT HAND OF DEXTRA

David J. Lake

DAW BOOKS, INC.
DONALD A. WOLLHEIM, PUBLISHER
1301 Avenue of the Americas
New York, N. Y. 10019

Cover art by George Barr.

Ophelia: Lord, we know what we are, but know not what we may be . . .

FIRST PRINTING, APRIL 1977

1 2 3 4 5 6 7 8 9

PRINTED IN U.S.A.

PART ONE:

Classica

Chapter One

The hydroskimmer from New Jerusalem slashed north like a knife over the still surface of Tethys Sea. The craft's motors changed the great silence to a harsh mechanical roar.

It was a warm day, and bright for a day of Dextra, with a gold sun-halo in the layer above layer of high cirrus. Under the diffused radiance, the people in the small ship could see the tideless waters stretching calm all the way ahead to the coast of Classica. Calm, and seemingly virgin.

A false seeming, thought Mark Turner. Here's one virgin who's been raped—or sacrificed.

The young biologist peered through the cabin's forward window at the dull milk-blue sea and the nearing green shore. He smiled grimly. The Appleseeders . . . they had sown with laser knife, with poison, with fire. Five hundred years ago, at First Landing, that shore would have been purple, not green; and that sea would have glowed, bright blue with phosphorescence. Tethys in her native glory . . . a bright virgin, girdled with purple. Now she was a captive to the invaders. Raped? No: half murdered. Only half: there was life in the slave girl yet.

Dammit, thought Mark, it'd be nice if we really *could* rape Dextra. Rape at least can fertilize. Those old conquests on Earth, when they led out the young women, the pretty girls as gifts for the winning army . . . how satisfying; those pretty little Midianites . . . a much nicer fate than Jephthah's daughter. . . .

Steady, he told himself. My metaphors—I know where they come from: my own damn frustration.

He glanced around at the others—the black-uniformed Navy men at the controls; the green-suited Science Agency personnel, most of them from Fisheries. Their business was murdering fish. At the moment the Fisheries men were clustered by the opposite side windows, but not looking at the scenery: their attention was centered on a girl. Mark's cousin Meriam seemed to be laying down the laws of Sociology as revealed in the Sifted Scriptures.

Mark smiled. Good old Meri. My-sister-my-spouse . . . well, that some day: and I don't suppose what she'll have to offer then will help me much. Meanwhile, good luck to the Fishers. With her, they'll need it.

He turned back to the book which lay open on the ship's table before him. He read:

> Take a planet.
>
> Take it when you are one hundred strong (or rather weak and weary), and are twenty empty years out from Man's native and only previous home. Take it when your great sub-light ship is wearing out its systems, and you can neither return nor voyage onward; and when, unaccountably, your radio pointed at Sol emits only eternal silence.
>
> Then let your planet teem with life, but no rational beings. Let it welcome you, warm from pole to pole like that Tertiary Earth, innocent of ice or

man, that we have all lost. Let it be in some ways a more earthly Earth, with the stars but dimly and seldom visible from its surface; its year, mass, and atmosphere like those of lost Earth, only a little more of each. Let your landers put down on the shore of its one great continent, and your people step gladly out on its blue grass, and walk among its purple trees and harmless beasts, and breathe the bittersweet air of that Eden, that New Earth.

Let some of them kneel, and give thanks to their invisible Lord.

And then let them all taste of the new fruits, the new fishes, the new meats—and find every form of living tissue totally and forever inedible, useless, irrelevant. . . .

"Mark, we're arriving!" said Meriam. She stood before him, a trim nineteen-year-old in green Agency uniform, dark-haired, dark-eyed, with sturdy legs and shapely thick ankles, pretty even in regulation boots, trousers and jacket. She sighed. "How typical of you to be reading! There's a time for that, of course, but now don't you think you should show a little Brotherhood for the others?"

"Well, it's Joshua's *Prolegomena to the Sifted Scriptures,"* said Mark defensively.

"Not the Scriptures themselves? Joshua is a bit suspect, you know. There's been a move in the House of Saints to ban him. Mark, I sometimes wonder if you're a true Lordist Saint at heart. Oh, I know you carry a Scar—"

"I couldn't wear this uniform if I didn't," said Mark. He was dressed almost exactly like Meriam and the Fishers, in the green of Good Life, only distinguished by the Hebrew and Roman letters of his breast-pocket insignia. He stood up and tucked the book into his grip. "Meri, dear, let's not quarrel. We're arriving, and we'd better put on a united front, we Livyans, when we go among the Classica heathens."

"You're right," said Meriam. Her expression softened, and she took Mark's hand. "Oh Mark—I am so looking forward to Classica! Such *wild* customs they have, the books say—but the notes add that not all the details have been recorded, especially in this recently settled eastern area. I could get such good material for my thesis! That was a most *fertile* idea of yours to take a working vacation abroad, a really *green* thought . . ."

Oh yeah, thought Mark, great: but when I mentioned it, I never dreamed you would want to tag along. Or that Uncle Jacob would let you. But I can guess your family's angle. . . .

They went on deck with their luggage, and took in the view. The Navy men were already mooring at a jetty, and the farm stead of Sunion, East Classica, confronted them at fifty meters' range. Farther down the jetty, on the other side, another boat was moored—apparently one of those *sail* craft. Beyond rose the land.

It was, Mark thought, just like the photos he had seen in his geography books at school in Livya—not only the pictures of the north shore of Tethys, but also of that legendary Old Classica of Planet Earth. Gray-green olive trees, pines, black cypresses—and on a rise a long low building in white stone, with pillars, arch, a vine trellis, and a low-pitched tile roof. Only . . .

. . . Only on a far ridge, about a kilometer inland, there was that curving line of purple which matched nothing in Earthly geography—the beginning of the native Dextran forest—the Frontier!

Mark felt a leaping excitement. Dextran native animals were his specialty, yet for many years now he had seen them only in zoo collections. He had never lived in a Province with a real Dextran Frontier before. Well, here it was, almost on his doorstep-to-be! He was glad now he had put in for this spot, the wildest, loneliest eastern end of Classica, the last human county north of Tethys. East of here was only the Narrows, and the Euxin Gulf, and unpeopled New Asia.

"Go with the Lord," said the hydro's captain, shaking each of them briefly by the left hand. "These Gentiles have been warned of your coming, and they will receive you courteously for fear of the Saints. Their Province Controllers make them keep rooms ready for passing Agency members—it is a condition for their holding the stead. Ah, here they come." He nodded to a group of people who were approaching along the jetty.

"That's all right, Captain Heber," said Meriam briskly. "We understand. The Lord bless you for giving us this lift."

"My pleasure," said Heber. "Power is too precious to waste—the Navy always likes to help out the Agencies on their lawful occasions. Now, my Fisheries passengers would like to be off about their godly work of smiting the enemy in the deep. If occasion serves, I shall call back here in a week's time to see that you are all right. Lord be with you."

Heber jumped back aboard, his black-jackets threw off the mooring ropes, and the skimmer's motors roared. Mark and Meriam dumped their luggage: one did not carry weight for a moment longer than necessary. And now, the Gentiles were upon them.

The Gentiles, though, did not seem alarming, nor to Mark's mind particularly wicked—only strange in their garb. Physically they were much like Livyans—most of them dark-haired and well bronzed by ultraviolet glare. There were two men, three women, and a clutter of children, also one teen-age girl and a dog. The people were dressed in white tunics, some also in colored cloaks, and the adults wore sandals. All were bare-legged, and the children barefooted.

Mark liked the look of the women. They were decked with aluminum bracelets and earrings. As they moved, they tinkled. They did not look like Saints.

"Sunion—population fifteen," said Meriam brightly and loud. "You seem to be nearly all here to meet us. The Anders family, I presume?"

A man, fortyish, dignified in a toga-cloak, stepped forward.

"Your census figures are most accurate, Mistress, but the figure should now be sixteen. Population Control will be glad to hear of another birth—and a boy at that." He indicated a black-haired, high-cheekboned young woman, who was carrying a small baby at her breast, unashamedly giving suck, her tunic unbuttoned. "One of my wives has borne a son."

"*One* of your wives?" Miriam bristled, obviously shocked and professionally intrigued at the same time. "But that's illegal now, isn't it—even here?"

"*Existing* bigamies are still legal in Classica," said the man stiffly. "I married Cynthia, my number two, before that last edict which FedCon forced our Province to pass. Gods! I remember the time when *our* Population Control was *encouraging* bigamies; and the sex ratio still isn't right. But enough of that: I must remember good manners, and keep off politics. You young people—you're not working for Federal PopCon, are you?"

"Our duograms should tell you otherwise," said Meriam, touching her left breast pocket. "Mine's Samekh-S: Sociology and Scripture. Mark is Beth-Z: a zoologist. We're cousins—same name, Turner—and our families have pledged us, because our genes check out. I mean, we're expected to marry. We're both on research grants from the University of New Jerusalem for the summer vacation. Oh yes, and my name's Meriam."

"Julian Anders," said the man. "I'm the steader."

Meriam extended her left hand, but Anders said, "No,

that's not *our* way—especially not with women. We're old fashioned," and he leaned forward and kissed her cheek. Then he gave his right hand to Mark. Mark took it awkwardly enough, but finally managed a dexter handshake.

Julian Anders now began introducing the rest of the extended family: his brother and chief assistant, Jason; Jason's wife, Doris, and her three children; Julian's first wife, Clio, and her four children.

"Clio has already achieved her legal minimum, you notice," said Julian. "Four live births. It's true only one is a boy, but we can't help that, so PopCon can't blame us."

"Master Anders," said Meriam, "we are *not* from PopCon, and I am sure you here are all doing your best to populate. I shall be facing the same problem and the same laws myself soon, I expect." She looked briefly, shyly, at Mark. "But let me tell you, in Livya we are working on this problem, this differential mortality—aren't we, Mark?—and we think we've got it beaten. It's largely a matter of prenatal care. The boys are more delicate, of course."

Mark was looking at Clio Anders and her teen-age daughter. Both were unusual for sixth-century Dextra; they were blond, blue-eyed, tanned, and tall. Clio's feet seemed to be hurting her—no wonder, thought Mark: she must be nearly 170 centimeters, and slim-ankled; if she'd been a male she surely wouldn't have survived to early middle age. Her type might have been viable on Earth, with 20 percent less gravity; but on Dextra, it wouldn't do. Tall slim-ankled blondes were rapidly becoming extinct.

He was glad, though, that the daughter, Helen Anders, wasn't extinct.

Seventeen years old, her father had said—but that was

by the funny old Earth-style reckoning they used for ages in Classica. By Dextran style, she was sweet sixteen. Well, not sweet exactly, but . . .

She was barefoot, her fair-bronzed feet were dirty and her tunic a little ragged, but she was nicely shaped, with a slightly sulky mouth. Not at all like what was available in New Jay, where indeed damn few girls were available. If this one would only look up: at the moment she was hanging her head, patting that dog . . .

. . . Which wasn't a dog. The creature now emerged properly from the group of children, and Mark saw, with a different but quite genuine pleasure, that it was a paracan—the six-legged native "dog" of Dextra. It was about the size of an earthly basset hound, squat and heavily built, black haired, with a huge, wide, toothy grin. Like nearly all Dextran mammals, its nose ended in three nostrils, left, middle and right.

Mark was immediately crouching down and making soothing noises to the beast. The paracan waddled up to him and began sniffing his hand. Finally, it licked his fingers.

"Why, he likes you!" said Helen, surprised. "Sextus usually doesn't. Like strangers, I mean."

Mark ruffled Sextus' fur, and his hand met Helen's, as if by accident. She did not withdraw it.

"Maybe it's because he can smell other paracans on me," said Mark. "No, I'm only joking. We can't keep native animals as pets in Livya, you know—but I wasn't born in Livya. Meriam was, but I wasn't. Both our fathers moved there, but mine moved later. *We* used to live in Atlantis—it's green and purple mixed up there—so I'm used to paracans, and other native creatures."

"You are?" said Helen. She was eyeing him almost hungrily. "Then I can show you many around here."

"I'd like that," said Mark.

They all moved off, tramping along the jetty. Julian had given the luggage to his womenfolk to carry, in spite of Meriam's protests.

"No, you're our *guests,*" he said. "That means something, in Classica. You say you've come to learn about our customs, Mistress Turner? Well, learn them. Even if you've been sent by our masters, the code of hospitality applies. Guests in Classica do not carry weights. Anyway, it's not far to some relief."

"But why do you make only the women carry?"

Julian adjusted his toga, and smiled. "Women are more durable. And we men have to take care of ourselves. There are fewer of us."

"In Livya," said Meriam coldly, "the rule is equality. Everyone works alike. And we have machines to take care of haulage."

"Machines?" said Julian. "We can't afford the fuel—or the metal. How is the minerals search going, by the way?"

"Not well," Meriam admitted. "Mem-S has found very little coal or oil lately, and no heavy metals at all. We are recycling everything possible, in Livya. We were lucky—I mean the Lord was good to us—in that we found all that iron in West Livya to start with, right after the Landing."

"Yes, that gave you your start over all the other Provinces," said Julian with a touch of bitterness. "And since the Coup—sorry, I mean since the Federal Government was transferred from Landing City to New Jay—well, I expect you can draw on the oil of Isthmia for your boats and things. Pity there's not enough metal and power for everyone! What's wrong with this damn planet? According to the histories, there was plenty of everything on old Earth."

"There was," said Mark, "and they wrecked the planet with it. Dextra's different, for several reasons. Heavy metals are rare because of our higher gravity—we've got 'em all right, but they've been dragged down to the core, out of the crust. Oil and coal—well, it's that good old 'purple' chemistry again. The Dextran organisms just didn't make so much usable stuff. But that's not too tragic—we can manage if we're careful. There's atomics, of course, but they're restricted."

"To New Jay," said Julian, "for some obvious reasons. Well, never mind—we can manage. We've learned to live off what the land affords. You see: here's our automobile truck."

They trudged onto the gray-brown soil of Classica, which here bore sparse Earthly grass. The "truck" was tethered to a pine tree: it was a hexip, the six-legged Dextran equivalent of horse, ass and camel. It had three nostrils, long ears, and short gray fur, and its feet ended in a cluster of three little hoofed toes on each extremity. It was sturdily built, and stood not much higher than an Earthly donkey.

The women now loaded the luggage into two pairs of panniers slung over the beast's backbone between each pair of legs. Then the boy Theseus, Julian's thirteen-year-old son, untied the hexip, took a stick, and began prodding the animal up the slope toward the family house. The hosts and guests followed.

Classica, thought Mark—it's beautiful. Even though the Appleseeders must've burned and poisoned all the native vegetation this close to the shore.

They plodded up the rise between an olive and a pine plantation. With the native blue grass had gone also the native microfauna: the olive trees were ringing with the electric whine of an Earthly cicada.

But there were still some wild strays. Yes, there went a Dextran flying beetle, huge and horny. The thicker atmosphere more than compensated for the higher gravity; this was a good world for flying things. The beetle disappeared out to sea, perhaps on some lonely migration past the Straits of Suez toward the lush shores of Hind.

And suddenly, there was a bird. If you didn't look too close, you could make believe it was an Earthly, tetrapod bird, an armless bird such as those which flew free in Livya's purely green and pleasant land. But Mark's expert eye picked out the pair of tiny clawed hands forward of the wings, the teeth in the half-open beak.

As he watched, the handibird plunged into an olive tree—and the cicada's song was silenced.

Silly idiot, thought Mark—what can he do with levoprotein?

Sure enough, seconds later the purple-feathered daymare (*Phantasma porphyropter*) emerged from the tree, spitting out shards of cicada and looking puzzled.

They trudged up the stone steps onto the spacious veranda—and suddenly Mark saw them. What he had been eagerly expecting for some time, what had brought him to Classica in the first place. Gobblers!

The little hominids seemed to have materialized out of thin air. Well, he knew they could move silently. They must have come from inside the house—and that was unexpected. Weren't they just farm beasts? Why . . .

"Meet the native help," said Julian Anders, with a satisfied smile. "Our house servants, no less."

Mark was staring, fascinated. Gobblers? Well, yes, more or less. Their behavior checked with the specimens he had studied—they were trembling with a sort of happy excitement, pawing the Anders children, waving to the grownups, and emitting that low musical burble that had won them their popular name. And, like the New Jay zoo specimens, they were erect tetrapods, blue-skinned, purple-furred, with four digits, pointed ears, anthropoid faces.

But no specimen Mark had studied had exceeded 120 centimeters in height. These were taller, their heads almost level with Mark's shoulders. Also, they were lacking in fur from the waist to the brow, so that they looked strikingly piebald: purple-furry below, blue above. And . . .

Lord of Landers, this was uncanny! In the chest region, they had distinct purplish nipples. Two of the gobblers were females, and these had slight but distinct twin swellings in the same area: blue breasts and purple nipples.

Mark gripped Julian Anders by the shoulder.

"Look—what *are* these? Are they really gobblers?"

"Not bad, eh? They're a new strain, just shipped in last year from New Asia, from Anthis in the Gulf. Cynthia's family, the Lees—they used to hold Sunion, but now they've moved east to Anthis, and set up a stead there. The farming there's not much, from what I've heard, but they've started a brisk trade in shipping over—well, gobblers, if you like, but I prefer to call this breed 'fauns.' I suppose we should call the females 'nymphs,' at that."

"Kind of cute, aren't they, the girl ones?" put in his brother Jason. "My wife Doris says they're so human, we ought to put clothes on 'em."

"But—but *nipples!*" said Mark. "Lord love you, Dextran mammals don't have external nipples! The milk glands are in the throat. These females don't use those *breasts* to suckle their young, do they?"

"No," agreed Julian. "Just like the older breed, the common gobbler, they chew up purple leaves and mix them with mouth-milk to feed their young imps. Yes, those false nipples *are* an oddity. My guess is that my father-in-law, Lucius Lee, has been doing some fancy breeding. He had some strange ideas, by the way—maybe you'll see signs of them around this stead. I've had to change things a bit since I took over. Among other things, push back the Frontier. You know the Classican saying, 'Purple is purple, people is people—and each in their own place'? I agree with that, all the way. I'm with you Saints to that extent. But fauns, now—if you treat them properly, they can be good servants. They're not very strong, but if you combine them with hexips—well, you can make a stead pretty well run itself. Now let's show you what my faun maids can do. Here—Topsy!"

Topsy came forward, mopping, mowing, and grinning. She had slit eyes, a very snub nose with two large nostrils, a thin, purple-lipped mouth, and a broad, triangular blue face topped by purple hair. Nevertheless, when grinning as now, she looked genuinely pleasant—a cheerful, friendly goblin.

"Topsy," said Julian, "you go with Mistress Helen, and Master Mark. This is Master Mark. OK?"

"O-kê," said Topsy.

Helen, who was carrying Mark's luggage again, handed over the lighter grip to Topsy. The purple-haired she-faun nodded over her blue shoulder.

"We go, chil'en," she said, and disappeared into the house carrying the grip.

Helen said, "She knows the way to your room, Mark. Come on."

Mark followed Helen into the house. He was a little stunned by what he had seen and heard.

Soon after the first discovery of the gobbler (genus *Satyrus*) two hundred years earlier, it had been ruled by GenCon, the Federal Government of New Earth, that the little purple-furred beasts were not rational animals. The intelligence of the known strains had been tested, and had come out at just about the level of the Earthly chimpanzee. But the gobblers had one great advantage over the chimp—they had a natural preadaptation to articulate speech, and so could be taught a few words of a crude pidgin English. The common gobblers had been in service in Classica as farm animals for the past fifty years. But no gobbler that Mark had ever seen had behaved in so civilized a fashion as Topsy.

They walked along a marble-walled corridor, then

turned right and entered the guest room. It was clean, large and airy, with plastered and frescoed walls, and wide windows looking east and south over the sea.

"Men's side of the house," said Helen, nodding at the windows. "We women have our rooms facing inland, toward the dangers, if any. Because we're expendable."

"Is there danger?" said Mark. "Helen—"

"Keep your cool," said the girl. "There's really nothing to worry about. We even have a fence, inland, to keep out leoids. This men's-side-women's-side thing is just a symbol. We can talk about that later. How do you like your room?"

"It's fine. Beautiful. We don't have painted walls like that in Livya."

He was staring at the fresco next to the door. It portrayed a curious scene. A half-naked young man, handsome and muscular, was reaching forward to seize a tearful naked girl—who seemed to be sprouting twigs and leaves on her fingers, bark on her skin, and roots on her toes. There was a sky background, impossibly blue.

"What in the world is it?" said Mark.

Helen laughed. "It's not in this world. It's a myth from Greece, Old Earth. Daphne turning into a tree."

"If it's supposed to be on Earth, then why are those leaves *purple?*"

"Oh, a touch of local color, I suppose." Helen shrugged. "Lucius Lee had that done—his eldest son, Endymion, painted it. I rather like it, don't you? And now, Mark, we're going to bathe you."

"What?" said Mark. There was already a noise of running water from the adjoining bathroom: Topsy must be in there.

Helen laughed again. "Old Classican custom. You know, the guys who founded this Province were a little crazy, I think—as crazy as you Saints in Livya, only the opposite way around. They were cultists too. Their idea was to revive the Good Old Days—the very old days of Earth. They also ransacked Scriptures—but different ones, not the Bible and the Koran, but Homer and Horace and so on. We're still saddled with Latin lessons on our Radio School—but maybe that won't last now that our ProvCon is under the thumb of GenCon, and GenCon is under the thumb of you people. Maybe it'll be Hebrew next year. But meanwhile, Mark—my father is a stickler for old Classican traditions, and it's one old Classican tradition for male guests to be bathed by the girls of the household, same as in Homer. Of course, if you object . . ."

"I do object. Meriam would have a fit."

"That might do her good. But if you object to a human bath girl, I can always leave you in the hands of Topsy."

Topsy at that poked her head out of the bathroom, a towel slung neatly over her blue arm. "Bath ready, chil'en," she said.

Helen sighed. "Topsy, not 'chil'en'! Mark and I—we're old, big. I've told you before. Call us Masters."

"O-kê, Mas'er Helly, Mas'er Mark. Mark, his bath ready now." Topsy approached, grinning, and touched Mark's jacket. "Mas'er Mark—he st-rip?"

Topsy was already unbuttoning the jacket. Mark flinched. He had never been in such a social, indeed intimate, relation to a specimen of *Satyrus* before.

"It's all right," said Helen. "She's quite safe. We leave the small children with them all the time—they make perfect nurses. Very friendly, very loving. Topsy will sit by your bath, hand you anything you want, scrub your back, rub you down in oil afterward—"

"No, please!" said Mark. "Not this time, anyway. Helen, I—I think your way of life here is charming. I'm not such a Saint as you might think! But give me time to get used to things. I'd like to take a good look at Topsy and her friends—but later, when I'm dressed."

Helen shrugged, said, "OK, see you," and withdrew with the she-faun.

As they went out, Mark was recalling that the sexual apparatus of *Satyrus,* both male and female, was extremely similar to that of *Homo.* He knew that if he had stripped in front of Topsy, he would not have been afraid.

He would have been shy.

The fresco on Meriam's wall depicted the Birth of Venus—a copy of an Old Earth painting. A tall blonde, very wistful and very naked, was approaching a lush forested shoreline, delivered, offered up to the world, on a large pearly seashell. On one side of her stood an ample, flowery lady; on the other side, a flying girl and boy, intertwined, naked, coupled.

Meriam blushed very red. "Oh Lord!" she said. "Cynthia, how can you live with such things?"

Cynthia Lee, twenty-one-year-old wife and mother, smiled serenely, and rocked her baby gently. The little boy was now certainly asleep, but she did not rebutton her tunic. "Very easily," she said, raising her strange black eyes. "After all, we can't live *without* them. Without doing them, I mean. So why object to having them painted?"

There was a sound of water running in the adjoining bathroom. Ah yes: that faun girl Mopsa. Poor little thing, thought Meriam, poor defenseless little slave. Naked, too. But perhaps that doesn't signify in her case. But these Classican women . . .

They sat on the bed side by side, Cynthia lulling her baby, Meriam unpacking her writing materials and books, and discarding her boots and socks.

"Don't you have anything to wear but a uniform?" said Cynthia, smiling. "And those *boots?*"

"We're not really on holiday," said Meriam defensively, "and when we're working, a uniform is what we wear.

And we travel as light as possible—so just one pair of our usual Livyan workboots."

What would the next move of the heathen be? To defend herself, she went over to the attack. (She ought to, anyway: this would count as sociology.)

"What's it like, Cynthia," she said, "what's it really like, being a second wife? Sharing your man?"

Cynthia shrugged—carefully, so as not to wake the baby.

"It's not what I would choose, if I had the choice. But there really aren't many nice men in East Classica. When my father moved out of here, I couldn't very well have gone with him—in Anthis, there'd have been nobody but my brothers. And Julian—well, he was taking over the stead, and I liked him, and I liked his wife Clio, and she didn't mind . . ."

"So Julian took you over too, along with the stead," said Meriam, forgetting sociology in simple indignation. "Oh, Cynthia! I'm sure I just couldn't . . ."

Cynthia smiled. "But then, you do things in Livya which *we* just couldn't. Like having your marriages arranged because of your genes."

"Oh, that," said Meriam, blushing. "Well, one can always object. In our case, it just seemed reasonable."

"Is Mark your lover?" said Cynthia. "Physically, I mean."

"Oh, *no,* of *course* not!" What things these Gentiles came out with!

"Why not? You're traveling together."

"But I *trust* Mark," said Meriam. "He's a *nice* boy. He would never . . . not till we're married!"

"Are you really sure of that? Anyway, would it matter?"

"Well," said Meriam reluctantly, "it's true that some Livyans are not very strict, if the couple get married after. My father, for instance. But my father's from Atlantis, anyway. On the other hand, my mother's a real Saint; she brought me up to behave decently."

"And Mark likes that in you?"

"Oh, surely," said Meriam. "He's never, *ever* tried to —to—"

"Then perhaps he's trying with someone else," said Cynthia evenly.

Meriam was too shocked to reply. And then Mopsa appeared.

"Bath ready for Mis'es Meri," she said, grinning.

"Please," said Meriam, turning to Cynthia. "Please, I'd like to bathe alone. Will you tell this little creature? But—but Cynthia, I'd like to talk to you afterward. Also to—to Clio your co-wife, and Doris, and that child Helen—"

"Helen's no child," said Cynthia, rising, "and I have a strong feeling she won't be available. I have these intuitions, you know, and they usually turn out to be correct. But you can talk to the others, and to my mother, Sybil—she's here, staying with us. Will that suit you?"

"Yes," said Meriam.

She had a leisurely bath. The bathroom was beautiful, all clean tiles, and the bath itself was a sunken one, very large and luxurious. Almost sinfully so—but that couldn't be helped, it wasn't her fault. It was pleasant to soak herself in the warm water . . . and think.

Cynthia was strange, she thought, very strange. Her eyes, the way she looked at you, those intuitions of hers . . . There was a word for that, in New Jerusalem. But what she said about Mark—that *couldn't* be true.

Could it?

Chapter Two

Mark had barely finished drying himself and had just got his trousers on again when his door opened and Helen stepped in. She had not knocked.

She did not waste words. "My mother and stepmother have got your Saintly cousin pinned down—they're discussing the Position of Women. Don't make the obvious funny remark! Look, it's an hour to dinner. Would you like me to show you the stead now?"

"Very much," said Mark, and got his boots on. He looked quickly at his grip lying on the bed. "Shall I bring my laser?"

"Gods, no. I'm not that dangerous!"

Mark laughed, and they both stole outside, down a small side passage and out by some back steps into the open air. They were now behind the stead-house, and could see items concealed by the traditional façade—the radio mast, the wind pumps, the solar-generator block. On their left, beyond a low stone wall, Mark noticed rows of cabbages, and Earthly poultry in a netted run.

"I see you haven't gone back to the old days altogether," he said, nodding at the radio mast.

"We compromise," said Helen, smiling. "There's enough power for electric light and radio, but not for Tri-Vee."

"Nice," he said, looking at the kitchen garden. "Why, that's not so different from Livya."

"Truly? I always thought Livya was a glorified sand spit, sticking out from Isthmia to Suez Strait—mostly a desert."

"That's how it was in the first century," said Mark, "but the Saints have done wonders there, you know. Perhaps its being a desert and a peninsula may have helped—there wasn't much Dextran life to eradicate. And now, with the industries and the irrigation, they've made the desert bloom like a rose—as *they* put it—an Earthly rose."

"Is it true there's no native life there *at all?*"

"Only in our labs and the university zoo. Even those I sometimes fear for, when some fanatic gets up in the Cube and calls for the 'complete purification of the Holy Land'!"

"What's the Cube?" asked Helen.

"The big Central Temple on Revelation Square in the middle of New Jerusalem. It's never *called* a temple, so as to fulfill a prophecy in the last chapter of Scripture. It's built as an exact cube for the same reason. New Jay is full of little gimmicks like that. Twelve township divisions in the city, twelve gates, and so on. The population target is a hundred and forty-four thousand, of course."

Helen stared. "One forty-four *what?*"

"Thousand. It'll get there in the next generation—we're already over the hundred-thousand mark."

"That must be quite, quite horrible," said the girl. "I was once in our Province capital, Eirenis—ten thousand people—almost every one of them strangers. I went nearly crazy. Oh, it was good for one thing, I suppose." She looked at him mischievously. "There were actually some unattached boys. They're hard to find in our neck of Classica." She broke off. "Here we are—the stables. I'll get you a saddle."

"What for? I can't ride one of those things," Mark protested.

"Then I'll teach you."

It was not quite as bad as Mark had feared. The riding saddle was perched forward of the hexip's middle pair of legs, and you could always grip the beast's neck in an emergency. After ten minutes or so, emergencies happened more rarely.

"Use your knees," said Helen, "and don't tug on the reins. There, that's better!"

"He does wiggle, though," Mark groaned. "I hope I won't be seasick!"

"Nonsense—he's as smooth as a crop buyer. All right—let's go!"

Their mounts broke into a brisk waddle, and Mark found himself riding beside Helen down a wide avenue. After a few minutes, the pines on either side gave way to open fields—on the right, tall green stalks of wheat, on the left, squares of blue and purple vegetation. Mark thought he could distinguish cereoids and parakale.

"Native food?"

"Yes," said Helen. "We grow it for our farm animals. Or rather, they grow it for themselves."

In fact, small blue figures were at work with hoes and hoses and wheelbarrows on both sides of the avenue. Some of them straightened up and waved to the riders. One field was bare earth, and a blue-skinned faun was leading a hexip through it, the beast drawing a small plow.

"Have you got *only* this type of gobbler around the farm?" asked Mark. "None of the full-hairies?"

"We had those till last year. Then, when we got these better ones, Uncle Jason sold off all the hairies to the steads farther west. These've made a terrific improvement. But that's enough of farming! I like this part of the stead better."

The fields were gone, and they plunged through a wood of oak and rhododendron and laurel. A great silence engulfed them. This was an Earthly forest, but it lacked Earthly wild animals, and Dextran ones could not or would not come into these alien glades and copses. No birds flew; not even a cicada sang. Nothing. It was almost uncanny.

Then they were out of the forest, at the edge of a new plantation of half-grown saplings. A couple of hundred meters beyond, on a rise, the purple woods of Dextra stood like the shield-wall of an ancient army defying invaders. The avenue passed on through the intervening half-grown green trees. But directly before them in the middle of a widening of the road there rose a strange tall stone statue.

"What's this?" said Mark, reining in his mount.

"D'you like it? Another piece of Lee artwork. Lucius designed it—that's Cynthia's father, you remember?" Helen vaulted nimbly to the ground. "Come and have a look. All right, I'll help you get off."

Mark had seen nothing like this statue in his whole life. It seemed to represent a four-armed woman rising out of an enormous, impossible flower. The flower itself was built on a fourfold plan, with series of four, eight, sixteen stone petals, and four great tendrils or tentacles rising up as though to engulf the woman. But the stone woman seemed not afraid, but herself fearsome. In her upper right hand she held forward a spherical fruit; in every other hand she held menaces—a dagger, a trident, a meathook. On her head, among writhing serpent tresses, she wore a crescent crown.

On the base of the statue was inscribed just one word:

HEXATE

Mark shuddered. "What in Hell is it?"

"Lucius never explained. He was a secretive character." Helen gazed at the statue, pondering. "Lucius designed it, and his son Endymion did the carving. Dymion sculpts, paints, writes poems. They're a strange family, the Lees. I like them. I even like my stepmother, Cynthia—

she's a Lee and she's strange and sometimes she can tell what's going to happen before it does. She said today she thinks Dymion will be coming here in the Lees' boat soon."

"I expect Endymion called her up on the radio."

Helen shook her head. "The Lees don't *have* radio—neither on their boat nor on their stead. Shows you how eccentric they are, doesn't it? Real *wild.* I like that."

"You like the wild?" said Mark.

Helen's eyes shone. "Very much. Let's go and see it, huh?"

She was pointing to the purple forest.

They remounted, and rode slowly forward through the low saplings. Helen explained about the new plantation.

"The Frontier used to be where the statue is, when Lucius was the steader here—four years ago. Only there wasn't any proper boundary then—the green and purple just merged. Then when my father took over, he burned back the wilderness, and put in these saplings—and built that fence."

They were up to it now: a high, solid fence of logs, two meters tall. Before it, just a few blades of insidious blue grass interspersed the Earthly green. Above and behind the rim of the topmost log, only a few meters back, rose the thick purple forest.

Mark imagined what it meant: up to this fence one kilometer of green, a tiny toehold of Man; but from this fence onward, three thousand kilometers of purple continent stretching all the way to the Arctic Mountains and the Northern Ocean.

"Can one get through?" he asked. "Right here—this looks like a door—"

"Sure is. But I didn't have time to steal the key." She looked at him, her eyes dancing. "Mark, I *would* like to take you there. And I will, first chance I get. But now, I guess we'd better go back. We'll be missed, and we'll be late for dinner."

Meriam found the Sunion women in the schoolroom by the back yard—an airy, whitewashed room equipped with little desks and chairs and a radio speaker now turned off. There was a blackboard on the wall, and a map of Classica, and on a table a battered old globe of Dextra standing with its usual 15-degree tilt. Meriam thought the whole setup extremely old-fashioned.

The ladies were seated by the walls on well-cushioned couches. They were apparently supervising the homework of half a dozen children, but in a relaxed manner, for they were also chatting quietly among themselves.

Here Meriam was introduced to Mistress Sybil Lee, Cynthia's mother, a woman with graying hair and strong features. Two of the children, a couple of little girls, were after all not Anders, but offspring of the absent Lee family of Anthis: they were staying here in Sunion under the care of their grandmother Sybil. In fact, everyone seemed rather under the care of Sybil: she dominated the gathering.

"Ah, my dear, so you are a young Saint?" she said, smiling graciously. "Do sit down and tell us about it. The children will be so interested! Come, little ones, no more Latin today. We'll have some sociology instead."

Meriam was a little amused to find herself for once an informant; but she was happy to give as clear a picture as she could of life in Livya. Of the subdivisions of New Jerusalem, each designed as a true community; of the countryside, with its commune-farms and its work camps in the mineral-bearing hills; of the cheerful meetinghouses, one in each parish, where the Scriptures were read on the New Sabbath, Monday, the Day of the Landing. Of the close-knit neighborly life of family and township and college and Agency; of the self-reliance and the loyalty, the decency and the severity of the Saints.

"I—I guess I'm not a real Saint, all the way through," she ended. "Not like my mother, or my mother's kin. Sometimes I even wish I lived in a more easygoing country—say, like Atlantis."

"Or like Classica?" said Clio Anders, smiling. "Meriam, dear, do you *have* to wear trousers and boots on your vacation? We could lend you something more comfortable. Like this." And she fingered her own light tunic. "As for *boots,* well . . ."

The women were all barefoot now: it seemed they did not wear sandals in the house. They all had elegantly painted toenails.

"Would you like some bangles and earrings?" said Cynthia. "Why, we could dress you up, give that Mark of yours a real surprise for dinner."

"I think *green* toenails would be appropriate for Meriam," said Sybil magisterially. "You know, the godly color. But you, children: this is becoming a grownup conversation. Lessons are over. Out you go."

The children left their books and scampered out into the yard.

"Well?" said Doris, Jason Anders' wife. "How about it, Meri? Shall we go to work on you?"

"Oh I couldn't, really," said Meriam. She felt pleased, though, and oddly excited. These "heathen" women were so nice! Very feminine . . . but that wasn't a Saintly ideal. If she *could* bring herself to give way to even *some* of their suggestions, whatever would Mark think of her?

But where *was* Mark all this while? It must be an hour since . . .

"You wondering where Mark's got to?" said Cynthia. "I can guess."

"I don't need to guess," said Clio grimly. "I haven't seen my daughter Helen since she was supposed to show him his room. You see, Meriam, Helen has been so deprived of male company for so long—"

"Not altogether," said Doris. "I caught her once with my Jason."

"What, her own uncle!" exclaimed Meriam, paling.

"Sure," said Doris, "and my Jason was quite, quite willing. But I got there in time—I think—and we've smoothed that one over. This is between us girls, you understand, Meri? We wouldn't like her father to know."

"Oh, I won't tell anybody," said Meriam. "I won't even use it in my work, since you've told me in confidence. Poor, poor girl!"

But already she was thinking, Poor, poor Mark. And—

And she herself felt wretched.

"I think—I think I might just borrow one of those tunics," she said.

Chapter Three

Dinner in Sunion began before the vague glow of the sun had sunk beneath the western hills. Mark and Helen were not really late, but they arrived last and together. Helen's uncle Jason made some broad jokes, and Mark became aware that Meriam seemed tense when they assembled in the large chamber that was the stead's main dining room.

"I was learning to ride a hexip," Mark explained. "Helen was teaching me."

"Is that all she was teaching you to ride?" chuckled Jason.

Mark avoided Meriam's eye.

At the same time, he mentally filed one pleasant fact: the Classicans were not jealous of their womenfolk; their limited polygamy had produced nothing like a harem system. In fact, the great Dextran imperative—to breed as fast as possible—had led to two different solutions in Livya and in Classica. The Livyans stressed breeding in optimum conditions, with strict monogamy and intensive care for children; the Classicans were inclined to let Nature take her prolific course. The other provinces—Isthmia, Atlantis and the West Coast—well, they were a muddle of both attitudes, but now tending to fall into the grip of the Livyan Saints.

Mark had been in the grip of the Livyan Saints all his teens, and now that he was twenty—nearly twenty-one—he regretted his misspent youth. Pity Meriam couldn't behave a bit more like Helen—but of course she couldn't. It wasn't in her. He'd known her casually since schooldays, and rather better since she too came to the university, and there had been this family-arranged betrothal. A good enough girl in her way, but a thorough Saint: she took after her pious mother.

And now she seemed to be getting a bit jealous. Luckily, they weren't going to sit together at dinner. In fact, nobody seemed to be going to sit at all. The Classicans reclined on couches at dinner, the men and women on opposite sides of the room, with small separate tables before the couches. On the wall there was a fresco of Bacchus and Ariadne, with hints of a drunken feast. It was all very sybaritic. Aha, how would Meriam take it?

Then he noticed, for the first time, that Meriam was wearing a Classican tunic, and sandals. The sandals were a bit big for her, and she was hobbling slightly. She must have borrowed this gear from the other women; she did look odd. The Classican ladies themselves were dressed for dinner more glamorously, in flowing gowns that left one shoulder bare. They had tucked up their feet on their couches, displaying their painted toenails.

When it came to the point, Meriam jibbed at the couches. "I don't think I can manage like that," she said, dismayed. "Couldn't I use a chair?"

Julian Anders shrugged. "Couches are a good idea, you know—take the weight off your feet and backbone. But have it your way, Mistress." He clapped his hands, and the blue-skinned little faun servants brought in a chair and placed it for Meriam beside the women's couches.

There were ten diners in all, for the small children were eating separately. Young Theseus counted as a grownup. Across the room, Mark noticed a woman of some fifty years, to whom he was now introduced.

"Mistress Sybil Lee," said Julian. "She preferred to stay here with us when her husband, Lucius, moved East."

Sybil's loose Classican dinner robe, Mark thought, did not quite suit her personality. She reminded him of many a Livyan matriarch.

"In case you are wondering, young man," said Sybil, "I am here, away from my husband, because I think he no longer needs me, and because I do not approve of his way of life. And Anthis is no place for a civilized family. I have managed to keep my grandchildren back from there, for the sake of their education—and for other reasons."

Mark said diffidently, "But don't their parents object?"

Sybil's jaw hardened, if that were possible. "Their mother may miss them, but she understands. As for my son Dymion—well, I think he's relieved. Without them, he has more scope—for various activities. He is a poet—of sorts." She smiled a little strangely. "Cynthia here says we shall be seeing him within forty-eight hours."

Meriam said brightly, "Imagine, Mark! Cynthia is a witch!"

"What?"

"Well, that's what the Elders would call her, back in Livya. The Lee family have this gift, most of them—it used to be called ESP in the old Prophane Science books." She turned to the others, and said apologetically, "I'm afraid ESP has been proscribed as nonsense—Scientific Heresy—that was decided at the First General Council of the Lordist Church. And one text was passed by the Sifters into our Scripture—'You shall not suffer a witch to live.' "

"You mean," said Julian, "in Livya they would put my Cynthia to death—just for talking nonsense?"

Meriam looked uncomfortable. "Oh, they would give her a chance to recant, you know. Then of course she'd no longer be a witch."

"And if she didn't recant?"

Meriam was silent. Mark said:

"The death penalty among the Saints is executed very simply. They just maroon you on an unconverted, un-Seeded shore—usually on an island in the Southern Ocean."

"How long would you last?" said young Theseus, agog.

"Depends on how long you want to drag it out," said Mark. "You could always drink the fresh water, of course. And there are other things you could get some nourishment from. You know Joshua's book, where he says that every form of Dextran life is 'inedible, useless, irrelevant'? Well, he was exaggerating—"

"Yeah, there's always wild wine," said Jason. "You could die happy-crazy, at that."

"Wild wine—exactly," said Mark. "Ethyl alcohol is a symmetric molecule—it is equally effective, whether you make it from our grapes or from native fruit. Of course, most varieties of wild wine taste hellish, because the minor ingredients are the wrong stereoisomers."

"Stereo what?" put in young Theseus.

"Haven't you got to that yet in radio school?" said Meriam. "Funny priorities your programmers have. Why, they teach us that in kindergarten in Livya. It's the most important single fact about our world."

"Hades," said Jason. "We're just simple farmers, in Classica. We know the difference between purple and green, though, without wrapping it up in fancy words."

Julian said, "Since you're a biologist, Mark, perhaps you can give us a little explanation of this stereo business."

"All right," said Mark. "I'll try to make it short and simple. The fact is, organic molecules have various important bits arranged in three dimensions. And most of these molecules come in two forms, which are mirror images of each other—three-dimensional mirror images, like your left and right hands. Ever try putting your left hand into a right-hand glove? Well, that's what it's like when a left-hand organism tries to eat right-handed food. No fit—no useful metabolism. The most important substances in our bodies—DNA, proteins—they come in the form which biologists have decided to call 'left-handed.' It was probably sheer chance that life arose on Planet Earth in the left-handed form—"

"In the Scriptures, it says 'such was the will of the Lord,'" objected Meriam, "and in the next verse, 'the Lord stretched forth his left hand.'"

"Well, it's likely that the Lord stretched forth either hand at random among the various lifebearing planets of the universe. My guess is that when life first arises anywhere, both left-hand and right-hand molecules are generated, and then there's a battle between them, and one or the other wins out. Long before the molecules reach the stage of true living cells, there's only one sort of protein or DNA. But it's just as likely that a planet will have right-hand life as left-hand life. This was a point that the Founders overlooked when they set out from Moon Base five and a half centuries ago. Their super-scopes had picked out a promising planet—but Dextra turned out to have only right-hand life—the wrong life from our point of view.

"So Dextran life forms are *nearly* all inedible to us. If you eat them, they taste bad, and they don't nourish you. But not many are actually poisonous, and you *can* use some of the sugars—because those are the same way around on Dextra as on Earth. But you can't live on sugar alone, indefinitely. If I were dumped on a purple island, I'd try just a few of the fruit—and after that I would have a go at fishing."

"What'd be the use of that?" said Helen, looking interested.

"Well, there'd be a slight chance of catching one of *our* fish," said Mark. "The seeded fry have been slipping through Suez Strait lately. Give the world another couple of centuries, and even Panthalassa, the World Ocean, will start to look like Tethys—the native algae crowded out, the phosphorescent diatoms deliberately poisoned by our Fisheries Agency, the native fish floating belly up like they do here. Well, by then maybe there won't be any purple life left on the land either. Some of the Saints are planning some pretty drastic schemes of chemical warfare."

Helen shuddered. "But why—why? Why can't they live and let live? There's plenty of space for both us and the native life."

"There is at present, yes. What's our world population—twenty-five million? Eight million in Livya, the rest clinging to toeholds on the edges of New Europe. If we take up all the other temperate shorelines, and the chilly Arctic, I guess we'll have room for a hundred million. But after that? We're doubling our numbers every twenty years now. In two hundred years, at this rate, our population will be twenty-five *billion*. We'll need every scrap of land on the whole World Continent and all the South Ocean islands—which are really too hot for human life anyway. Then maybe some maniac will try to fulfill literally that text in Scripture, and finally terraform New Earth—and there will be *no more sea.*"

"It can't possibly come to that," said Julian.

"It nearly came to that on Old Earth," said Mark, "before they blew the whole place up, and had to survive on the Moon till they could send off the starships. It *could* come to that here. Unless some day not too far ahead we have PopCon in reverse, and women won't be *allowed* to have as *many* as four children."

"Mark, what an unholy idea!" exclaimed Meriam. "Isn't it written in the Scriptures, the very first chapter, 'Increase and multiply, and fill the new Earth, and subdue it, and have dominion over the fish of the sea and the fowl of the air and every living thing that moves upon the land'?"

"It is so written," said Mark bitterly. "That's the prime text of Lordism, I agree—the Lord will help us all to be Lords of the world. Myself, I prefer that verse in the Sifted Koran—'The Lord set the Balance of all things, that you might not transgress it.' "

"That refers to justice," said Meriam, "not ecology—as you ought to know, Mark. The Midrash—"

"If you'll excuse us, young people," said Julian smoothly, "this theological discussion is rather above our heathen heads. I'll give you a text, too, if you like, out of our own Scriptures—'You may drive out Nature with a pitchfork, but she'll always come back at you.' Well, Nature at the moment is reminding me that I'm hungry. Let's eat."

It was a good meal, beginning and ending with plenty of fruit, and taking in on the way bread, olives, roast chicken, and fresh Earthly fish drawn from Tethys. The faun servitors brought everything, handling plates and baskets with grace and four-fingered dexterity.

"They even caught this fish," said Julian, as he poured the wine out of an earthen jar into the mixing bowl. "Clever little beasts, aren't they? We send them out in boats, all by themselves, and they're very good with hook and line."

Mark took a deep draught of his wine cup. "Er—isn't there any danger they might escape?"

"Escape? To where?" said Julian. "Gobblers never have been native in New Europe. Both strains come from the East, from beyond the Euxin, and as I say Dymion brought this lot from Anthis and sold them to me last year. They don't show any signs of wishing to leave us. They're quite happy here."

"Weren't they upset at being shipped over the sea and sold?" asked Meriam. "They seem so intelligent. Having them about the house—it's so like what the old books say about early Planet Earth. You know—*slaves.*"

Julian smiled. "Yes. *Old* Classica simply couldn't have been run without slaves, human slaves. The gobblers—and my fauns—they are the indispensable substitute. But these fauns don't behave like human slaves. Dymion says they're positively eager to be shipped. Maybe there's something they're afraid of in their native land, that they're escaping from by coming here."

"But selling them," said Meriam. "Doesn't that split up—er—families?"

The Anders men roared with laughter. Mark coughed.

"The genus *Satyrus* doesn't go in for family life, dear," he explained. "They're totally promiscuous, like Earthly monkeys. They have an estrus cycle, too. At least, that's true of the earlier strains. Is it the same with these—fauns?"

"Yes," said Julian. "But why do you talk of 'earlier strains'? I thought there was only one other sort, the full-hairy common gobbler."

Mark cleared his throat. The meal was ending, and the

wine jar was circulating. Twilight had deepened, and the little servants had turned on the electric lights, a few dim bulbs on side tables tastefully concealed in mock Roman mock oil lamps. Mark said, "Shall I tell you what brought me to Classica?"

"By all means," said Julian. He hefted an empty wine jar, and called to a male faun. "Here, Gollibub, bring us another, boy."

The faun bowed, took the jar, and whisked out of the room. Presently he brought the replacement and left. Mark looked after him.

"I'm on the trail of just those creatures," he said. "They're a terrific anomaly, and what I've seen today only makes the anomaly ten times worse." He paused and fished a couple of photos out of his pocket. "Look, Master Anders, what do you make of these?"

Julian studied the pictures. "One's a common gobbler—a full-hairy. But what's the other? It's a bit like a gobbler—but it's got three nostrils, and a tail, and it's ugly as Hades—face more like my dog Sextus than any gobbler or faun."

"Quite so," said Mark, "and what the picture doesn't make clear is that it was *small*. Barely a meter tall, if it stood upright—which it usually didn't. Will you pass the pictures over to the ladies? Thank you." He paused; then, when they had all seen the photos, he said:

"Well, folks, that little monster was *Satyrus tetradactylus*—the first species of gobbler, discovered two hundred years ago by a scouting skimmer's crew on the shores of Anthis, New Asia. Several specimens were brought to zoos in New Europe and Livya, but they all died quickly in captivity.

"Mind you, they were already a startling anomaly. A native *tetrapod* animal! As you know, practically every land vertebrate on Dextra is hexapod—which is only reasonable, considering our gravity. I sometimes wish we *humans* had six limbs—two arms, OK, but four legs would be a godsend in 1.25 standard gees. Of course, gobblers aren't much inconvenienced by the gravity, because they're small—they have less weight to support on each square centimeter of footsole. But how did they come to be four-limbed?

"The first guess anybody produced was that they had originated on another continent. All the native hexapods are derived, ultimately, from marine octobrachs—those eight-pointed starfish things you pick up on the beach. Half a billion years back the octobrachs came ashore—two arms developed a backbone and became a main body, the other six arms became vertebrate limbs. But if there had been a second continent, quite isolated from this one, then there could have been *another* shore-clambering—perhaps by a fish with four strong fins, as happened on old Earth."

"There's just one snag to that idea," said Jason. "There doesn't happen to *be* any second continent."

"Oh, but there is," said Mark. "In fact, there are two. Only, since Dextra has more water than Earth, they're submerged. One is totally so—that's the Lemuria Bank, in the middle of Panthalassa, halfway around the world. There's not even a mountain peak sticking up there to give us an island, but it's a real continent all the same. The other one is Gondwana—that collection of jungle islands in the south equatorial belt, southeast of Hind. Now, there's evidence that Dextra has not always been this warm—we've found traces of at least one Ice Age—so with water locked up in ice, both Gondwana and Lemuria could have been real land continents at one time. So that 'original tetrapod' theory was just feasible. The trouble was, we couldn't find any other tetrapods—bar a few pseudos: flightless birds, island forms that had lost their midlimb wings."

"So what's the answer?" asked Julian.

"We're almost sure now that gobblers are basically flightless Mesoptera—former bat-monkeys. Everything else in the skeleton corresponds—but it's odd that there's no vestige of the middle limbs. Even we humans have a vestigial tail skeleton at the end of our spine! But in the gobblers—nothing: the middle limb skeleton has been removed utterly, as though it had never been. And—this is where I come to round two of the mystery—exactly the same thing happened later to the tail—under our eyes, so to speak."

"You mean, between these two stages," said Helen, getting up and laying the photos before Mark.

"Exactly." (As bright as she's beautiful, he thought.) "Gobbler number two appeared one hundred years ago—again, in Anthis. You know what they're like—the common gobblers—they're more human-looking than the first sort, bigger, erect, with not the slightest sign of tail or tail skeleton, and with only *two* nostrils." Though the evening was warm, he shivered. "That should've set people wondering, but somehow it didn't. I guess our science has been too practical for too long. The new gobbler was simply docketed as a newly discovered species. This planet still holds plenty of surprises—since we gave up air transport as too costly in power, we've been doing nothing but skim coastlines, and the interior of the continent may hold all sorts of surprising beasts. Not many people care *what* there is, so long as it's not dangerous. And gobblers obviously aren't. The new species was named *Satyrus erectus,* and we filled our zoos with it and finally you Classicans used it as a farm helper. This species was hardy—it throve in captivity.

"I myself only came upon the *Satyrus* problem recently, during my graduate work. What really shook me was this: there've been a number of voyages to Anthis lately, and they have duly found gobblers—but *all* were of the second species, *erectus*. Not a single specimen of the earlier tailed version, although those seemed to be common, according to records, two hundred years ago."

"Maybe the bigger gobblers gobbled up the small ones," suggested Jason.

"Uncle, no!" cried young Theseus. "They *wouldn't!* They don't even eat meat!"

"True," said Mark, "but you may have a point there, Jason. The big species could have made the small one extinct merely by competition for food and territory. That's what I'd like to know about. I had in mind to pick up what information I could here, and then—but now, today, what do I find? Round three! Type three! Your new fauns are bigger again, and a bit more humanoid again—false *nipples,* for the Lord's sake! What's going on in Anthis?"

Sybil Lee, the old matriarch, smiled grimly. "Well may you ask, young man. As for myself, I do not think I wish to know."

"But *I* wish to know—very badly." Mark turned to Julian. "I don't want to slight your hospitality, Steadmaster, but if I could find transport to Anthis—"

"Very likely you can," said Julian. "If Dymion does turn up—and really he's due soon anyway, apart from Cynthia's mental radio—well, I'm sure you could sail back with him."

"Travel in a sailboat—over the Euxin!" said Meriam. "Why, it must be a thousand kilometers!"

"It is," said Julian, "but Dymion's done it frequently. Takes five, six days usually. Flora—that's the Lees' stead—it lies right at the end of the southeast gulf. Most of the way, you coast the north shore of Anthis."

"But isn't it dangerous?"

"Many things in life are dangerous," said Julian drily, "like marrying, or running a stead, or putting up Agents from New Jay, who aren't always nice simple honest folk like you young people. All I can say about that sailboat is, Dymion hasn't been drowned yet."

"Mark, would you really go?" said Meriam. "We might get a skimmer some time—"

"There's no service to Anthis," said Mark. "And no expedition is currently planned. You know I checked! Yes, I will sail with Dymion Lee, if he'll have me."

Meriam was silent. And now, at a signal from Julian, the womenfolk rose and, following Classican custom, retired from the dining room, leaving the men sitting over their wine.

"What's it like in New Jay for a young feller?" said Jason with a wink. "Come on, Mark, tell us what the Saintly girls are like when you catch them away from their mothers. Same as any other girls, I bet, eh?"

Mark murmured that things weren't quite like that; and there ensued a conversation that he found rather boring. After the shortest decent interval he got up, saying he was tired. He could do with a good sleep.

"Then you'd better lock your door," said Jason, with a guffaw.

Mark did not lock his door. He had hardly turned off the light when he heard a soft, hesitant knock.

"Come in," he called, not too loud, his heart thumping.

The room was dim in the faint glow of the wide windows. A figure came in, moving with the soft slap-slap of bare feet on stone floor. He rose to meet her, anticipation glorious already in his loins. Then she spoke.

"Mark—"

"Oh, *no,*" he groaned. It was Meriam.

"Mark, I wanted to talk to you. I just hoped you mightn't be too long with those men. You weren't asleep already, were you?"

"No. Shall I put on the light? It's so warm, I'm only wearing sleeping shorts."

"That's quite decent, dear. And I'm wearing a Classican tunic—the women lent it to me. You don't mind that, do you?"

"No," said Mark coldly. "Whatever you wear, Meri, you know your virtue will be safe with me."

"Oh," she said, and made an odd little noise, like a gulp.

"Shall I put on the light?" he repeated.

"No, don't bother—it's only a waste of their power. Come, let's sit by the window."

Mark drew up a stool for Meriam, and himself sat on the edge of his bed. The faint phosphorescence of dying Tethys plus the tiny glow of a couple of Dextra's small moons gave them enough light to see each other, more or less.

"Mark," said Meriam, "what do you think of Classica, so far?"

"It's beautiful. Fascinating. The animals—"

"Not *just* the animals, surely?" Meriam gave a little laugh. "Incidentally, Helen saw me coming here, so you needn't strain your ears—I think she'll at least wait till I'm gone. I suppose you realize that that girl's sex-crazy? I—maybe I shouldn't ask you, but—have you done it with her, already?"

"No, no, what do you think—"

"Oh Mark." This time she certainly gulped: it was half a sob. "I suppose I've been silly. Perhaps it doesn't matter; I don't know about boys. Perhaps you have to get it out of your system—if so, I don't really mind. So long as nothing really comes between us in the long run, dear—because I'm fond of you. And—"

"And what?"

"I don't know how to say this, exactly. Classica's very seductive—not just Helen, the whole thing. Don't think I don't feel it myself—I'm not made of wood, you know. The women—especially Sybil—there's a graciousness about them, and they have been very, very nice to me."

"So you don't think they're all just wicked heathen, then?"

"Not all of them, no. I don't care for the men, and that Cynthia's at least a bit weird, but Sybil's a fine person, and the children are delightful, and those fauns—they're ducky! Mark, that's what I really came to talk to you about."

"The fauns?"

"Yes. Mark, when we get back to New Jerusalem, we must do something about them."

"What do you mean?"

"Mark, do you approve of slavery?"

"No, of course not. But GenCon ruled that gobblers we not rational—"

"You know that's wrong—or if it was right about the earlier gobblers, it certainly *isn't* right about these ones, these fauns. These Classican men are just too insensitive to see it, or maybe they don't want to see it. Mark, just now I actually had a *conversation* with one of the faun girls. Her name was Mopsa, and she was sweeping out my room. I said, 'Are you happy to be working here, Mopsa?' And she said, 'Yes, Mis'es Meri, I be very happy—Anders Mas'ers 'n' Mis'eses very nice.' If that's not an intelligent conversation, I'd like to know what is."

"You're right," said Mark. "But you heard what the girl said—she was happy. Look, Meri, you're a sociologist. You must know that every society is a *system*. Let's not start interfering with this one till we know all the elements that make up the system. Above all, till I've been to Anthis and solved this mystery of the fauns' origin."

"Till *we've* been to Anthis, you mean."

"What, are you coming too—on that sailboat?"

"Of course, my lord and husband-to-be. There are people in Anthis, aren't there? Even wilder Classicans, so it seems. I could do research on them."

"But that's not your real reason," said Mark, irritated.

"It's this 'whither thou goest, I will go' thing, isn't it?"

Meriam was silent a moment. Then she said softly: "I think I just *could* be some use to you, Mark, in those wild parts. Of course, if you don't want me . . ."

"Oh, don't be silly," he said, standing up. "Of course you can come."

She rose too, and kissed him lightly on the cheek. Then she moved away, and slipped out of the room. He heard again the faint slap of her footsteps, and remembered that she had been barefoot. Astonishing: Meriam had always worn at least slippers indoors before.

What was up with his cousin? Up to now, she had been so predictable. And she had hardly ever discussed their future marriage, except as a placid certainty.

Hell, thought Mark, I hope she's not going to be difficult.

He remained awake for some time, half hopeful of another visit: but Helen did not come to him that night.

Chapter Four

When he opened his eyes, it was morning, and the little faun Topsy was standing over his bed, her broad blue face wreathed in a cheerful grin.

"Mornin', Mas'er Mark. You like coffee?"

"Very much."

Topsy whisked out, and soon returned not only with coffee but also with Classican pastries and oranges—in fact, breakfast. She stood by grinning while he ate. Even before he had finished he began questioning her. He was soon sure that Meriam was right—the fauns *were* a rational species. But Topsy had only the vaguest notions of her people's history.

"Come over sea," she said, "from de place of big big plants."

"The forests?"

"Right, Mas'er Mark—de fores'. De fores' is our mammy."

"Are there smaller ones like you in that forest? I mean, grownup gobblers, but only so high?" He held his hand level with his waist.

Topsy shook her head. "All grow same. Same as me."

Almost literally true, thought Mark. He had noticed it already: there was astonishingly little range in height and bulk among adult fauns. Both sexes stood 130 to 135 centimeters tall—neither more nor less. Well, he'd better check that today—check all the fauns on the stead, measure and weigh the smallest and biggest, examine those false nipples minutely, record everything. Yes, but there'd be ample time for all that. Meanwhile, he had other needs. . . .

"Where is everybody?" he asked. "The family, and—and Mistress Helen?"

Topsy told him. The Anders were out and about already. The men had ridden out to a maize field near the eastern boundary of the stead, to supervise some faun workers there; most of the ladies were out gardening, and Meriam was with them.

"But de kids be down at de jetty lookin' over de sailboat," said Topsy, "and Mis'es Helly is wid *dem.*"

The Anders' sailboat was of the best Classican kind, built at no small cost by the Eirenis shipyard to serve the farmers' need of coastwise transport. It was of a design developed on Dextra, to minimize crew numbers. The plastic sails could be spread and "furled" by activating a little electric motor in the control cabin—the sails simply slid out of the hollow dural masts, pulled by the powered wires, and were spooled in again when not needed. No one had to "go aloft"—which would in any case have been a hazardous operation in Dextran gravity.

"You'd only need two or three to sail this boat of ours," said Helen, "and not all of them need be humans. One day I guess we'll train the fauns to skipper her and do the whole navigation." She laughed. "But if you go on the Lees' boat, you'll find things different, even though it's cunningly rigged. Dymion and his kid brother built it themselves, with wood and ropes—it's an old Earth type. 'Course, it's cheaper and cheaper to run than ours, but it does run more slowly." She looked Mark straight in the eyes. "Had enough of this, now?"

"Yes," he said. Theseus and the other children were some way down the deck, out of earshot.

"Then let's take another ride. Go up and wait for me by the stable." Her eyes danced mischievously. "I think I can get hold of that key now."

"The key to the Frontier fence?"

Helen nodded.

"In that case," said Mark, "I'll call in at my room, and get my laser."

"Oh, if you like." She shrugged. "Leoids aren't very common, you know. My uncle Jason has been riding out every so often to shoot them—for sport. But he's bagged very few over the last three months."

"Still . . ." said Mark; and went.

The weather was beautiful that high morning—not too hot for nearly midsummer, and not too overcast. Only the cirrus wreathed up and up to the threshold of the stratosphere, and the gold sun-halo slid from crisp curl to curl of ceiling cloud.

The ride through the plantations was exhilarating. Mark felt he had thoroughly mastered the art of staying on a hexip, and so he had leisure to observe things around him. The fauns in the fields were at work as usual—and now beside one field he saw a couple of small mothers with tiny faun babies. These were furless down to their toes, delightful little blue manikins. They were already able to stand, and their mothers were mouth-suckling them—it looked like mouth-to-mouth kissing.

But this reminded Mark of his zoological duties, and he turned to look at Helen instead. He had admired her at dinner the previous night in her off-one-shoulder gown; now she was back to her short tunic. As she rode, the tunic also rode—up very high, exposing the lower edge of her undershorts, and also nearly all her sun-kissed thigh, not to mention her slim golden lower leg and bare foot. He licked his lips.

"Do you go in for sunbathing?" he said.

"Not much—I wish I could, but my skin's too fair, I would burn. But I do swim a bit."

"What do you swim in?"

"The sea."

"No, I mean what sort of clothes do you use? The Livyan bathing suit covers nearly everything."

"I don't use clothes at all," said Helen calmly. "No one does, here."

"Oh," said Mark, his heart thumping, and wondering how to suggest a swimming party.

They left the fields behind without coming across any humans, and plunged into the holm-oak wood. This time, the cicadas were singing.

"This is marvelous," cried Mark, as they trot-wriggled along the shaded avenue. "I wish I had learned to ride when I was a boy in Atlantis. They do have hexips there, you know."

"What's Atlantis like?" said Helen.

"Better than Livya! The green and the purple grow side by side, and there's plenty of wildlife. It's lush country, cool and wet, and the Western Ocean glows at night—that's still nearly pure native. It's bright blue by day." He sighed. "But we left there when I was twelve. My father was a mining engineer, and he was attracted to the work that was going in Livya. He wasn't a Lordist then, but we all had to become Saints later—you're really nothing in Livya if you're not one. My mother came to take the religion seriously—nearly as much as Meriam's mother—but my father and I never did. Dammit, how can you take seriously a religion that was invented by a committee?"

Helen laughed. "Did they really invent it? I thought the Lordists claim they merely purified the old Jehovah religions of Earth."

"They pooled them," said Mark, "and threw out what didn't suit their needs, and partly rewrote some of the texts. They put in a 'new' here and there before the word 'Earth,' and changed 'right hand' to 'left hand' to fit in with our sacred proteins. Hence our Livyan left-handed handshake. The whole thing was carefully and coolly planned by sociologists—that's why Sociology and Scripture are still one Agency. Of course, after a couple of generations the products of the system really believed it was sacred. They've forgotten that from the start it was all slanted—to give humans a blank charter to conquer this planet in the name of the Lord. The Lord, by the way, is now pictured as a clean-shaven elderly guy in a green uniform like the one I'm wearing now."

"Oh well," said Helen, "I suppose everyone creates his god in his own image."

"Really? Then what about *that?*"

They had come to the open space, and were confronted with the statue of Hexate. Mark stopped riding.

Helen also checked her mount, and stared at the statue. In her eyes there was awe, almost love.

"It's a very Lee-family thing," she said slowly. "I can't explain it, but I feel it. See how *rooted* she is, that six-limbed woman. She's a real native."

"She's not a faun, though."

"No." Helen sighed. "Mark, what must it have been like on Planet Earth—in the very oldest of old days, when humans were just beginning, when they were just about as bright as fauns! Then they stood up naked on their own mother planet—what we can never do." She laughed. "That reminds me of a poem Dymion Lee made up last year. It was so crazy I couldn't forget it. It's not long. Would you like to hear it?"

"Please."

Helen caressed her hexip's neck, and recited:

"Once I knew a native,
her name was Naomi:
naked was her navel,
such was her nature.
Such is the nature
of all stark natives.
O man, conquistador clothed in your God
armored, invincible, waterproof, shod—
Be mindful of Naomi,
she is your neighbor:
we once were all naked
in mother Nature,
navel to navel
all we stark natives.

"A real crazy poem, no?"

"It sure is. Who was Naomi?"

"Well, Dymion had a faun of that name, one that he

sold us. She wasn't anything special, though. All fauns are much alike."

"I've noticed that," said Mark. "Shall we be getting on?"

They rode through the young pines and reached the fence. Helen dismounted, tied her hexip to a sapling, and then produced a large key from the pocket of her under-shorts.

The wooden door swung open. Outside was a short stretch of native blue grass, and then the dark trunks of the Dextran forest.

"You can ride your beast through," said Helen.

"What about yours?"

"I'll leave him here. They're very strong, you know: yours will carry both of us. I won't need a saddle—I'm used to riding them bareback. I'll get up behind you."

"All right," said Mark, and went through.

Helen came after him, locked the door from the outside, and vaulted into the place between the hexip's midback hump and its rear pair of legs. The beast grunted, and began moving forward.

Helen clasped her arms round Mark's waist. "Here we go," she said. "Ride, Mark!"

The forest loomed up and embraced them.

It was the scent that first struck him with nostalgia—it was like the woods of Atlantis, only more so, more aromatic, a bittersweet smell compounded of certain native leaves, bark, and flowers with not quite the right sort of perfumes—or rather, with precisely the *right* sort, unfit for the noses of left-handed life. And yet not truly unpleasant: alien, other, exotic.

The going was not difficult, because there was no thick underbrush, merely sparse blue grasses and occasional bushes of huge and brilliant flowers—red, orange and yellow blooms as big as a man's head perched on thick blue stalks. The trees were thick-trunked too: squatter than Earthly trees, they seldom rose more than seven or eight meters above ground, their dark, almost black wood boles strangely bulbous near the bases. Some sprouted in multiple trunks, like Earthly banyans; one species rose on four regularly arranged black stems like the legs of an elephant, which united at a little over head height to form a main body nearly a meter across, and then threw up four main branches that lost themselves in a canopy of black twigs and purple leaves.

"The greater mandrake," murmured Mark, riding his hexip between and under the tree's 'legs.' "They look spooky, don't they?" Indeed, many of the trees and some of the lesser plants looked like queer parodies of men or other animals: you could fancy that when you had ridden past, they would start picking up their black woody feet and sidling off to better locations.

Which of course was nonsense. "Ooh, don't scare me!" cried Helen in mock alarm, and hugged Mark more tightly round his jacketed waist—which he did not mind at all.

There was plenty of genuinely mobile life in the forest, both on its blue floor and in its purple ceiling. Great beetles whirred, and toothed handibirds pursued them. As they crossed one small glade, a bat-monkey took off and sailed across the open space, his midlimb wing flap extended, his underbelly pale gold against the pale gold cloudy sky. And among the blue bushes of the same glade, they suddenly flushed out a flock of centauroids—small deerlike creatures which had been plucking orange fruit with their delicate four-fingered hands.

Helen cried out with delight. "Oh, how lovely they are, those little chaps! Like the centaurs in the old books, but neater. They're pretty smart, too: they've learned to keep out of our way since Jason came here with his laser rifle."

"What, does he shoot *those?*" Mark was shocked. "We can't eat them!"

"He calls it *sport*. I used to like my uncle Jason, but I

don't much now. There might've been some excuse for shooting little centaurs before we had the fence, because they're partial to golden apples—you know, what we saw them eating just now—and we grow some of that for our native help. But now there's no excuse at all. I love centaurs. Mark, how is it there aren't any rational ones?"

"I couldn't say. That problem applies right across the board with Dextran mammals. So many species are equipped with useful hands—if it's manual dexterity that produces intelligence, they ought to be geniuses! But my guess is, there are other factors. You can't think accurately without words, and not many species have the right sort of vocal apparatus—in fact, only the gobblers seem to have exactly what's required there. Mind you, many Dextran mammals are pretty bright—several come up to the Earthly chimp level, or higher. It's the dolphin problem over again, I guess—what do you mean by intelligence?" He laughed. "Maybe they're too smart to try speaking. That's an old Earth legend about one type of primate—if they started speaking, we'd grab them and put them to work, like the gobblers. As it is, they get along fine, these centauroids. With two hands and four feet, they're perfectly adapted to this planet."

"I wish I was like them," said Helen.

"Eh?"

"I wish *I* was adapted to this planet. I wish I didn't have a fair skin, I wish I could eat fairy food—"

"Fairy food?"

"Sorry, that's Classican slang for purple stuff. You know, it's like the fairy food in Earth legends, it doesn't nourish us. But it does nourish the centaurs. They're lucky in so many ways! They don't get sunburned, they don't weigh too much. I wish I could say the same of myself. I'm too tall, and I weigh too much, and my ankles are too slim. An old-fashioned Earthly type. Hades, I wish I had four feet! Like you said, there'd be less weight on each one. And I could move a lot faster."

"Why do you go barefoot?" said Mark. "Doesn't it hurt?"

"No more than in shoes. I'm used to going barefoot—I always have, from a little kid. They made me wear shoes when I went to Eirenis last time, and I hated it. Hot and hurtful. Besides, I like to feel Dextra between my toes." She paused. "Here, Mark, let's get down."

They had come to an edge of the forest, and what lay before them was a blue plain dotted with purple trees. In some directions, the horizon looked enormously far. Directly ahead Mark reckoned he could see for nearly five kilometers before the ground rose and the trees thickened again. Over the grass, in the distance, he could see herds of large animals—hexabos, bigger centauroids, with here and there the moving dots which must be lurking predators, wild paracans, feloids, tyrannotheres. Overhead wheeled hexeagles and paravultures. It was a spellbinding sight—something like a plain full of big game on Earth before Man fouled up that planet.

They dismounted. Mark felt for his laser pistol, making sure it slid easily in its holster.

Helen laughed. "The predators couldn't care less about eating us. They've got good noses, they can tell we're the wrong sort of meat."

"I know," said Mark. "Still, I'm the cautious type. You never know what might happen."

Helen was tying the hexip to the nearest tree. She looked at Mark, and wrinkled her nose.

"You're still scared of Nature in the raw, aren't you, Mark? Those Livyan Saints have affected you more than you realize, I think."

She left the hexip, and moved to a bank of short blue grass half surrounded by bright-flowered bushes. Here she sat down, and patted the ground beside her. "Come on, sit by me. This is a good place."

Mark obeyed.

"Try taking off those silly boots," said Helen. "This grass is beautiful underfoot."

Mark removed his boots and socks, and felt the blue vegetation between his toes. It was soft, with a hint of moisture. "Yes, nice," he said.

"Just think," said the girl, "if only we had the right chemicals in us, Mark, we wouldn't have to live behind that fence *at all*. We could roam those plains and live off the country—all three thousand kilometers of it, chasing the hexabos like those redskins of Earth with their buffalo." She looked out at the plain, her eyes dreamy, soft and blue.

And he looked at her. She was very close, with her bare gold-tanned arms, legs and feet, and her fair hair lay tousled about her face, and she smelled good.

"We—we couldn't run fast enough to catch hexabos," said Mark. "Helen, I—"

"What?" She turned and looked squarely at him. Then she laughed. "Mark, when did you last have a girl?"

"I always have a girl. Meriam."

"I don't mean that, silly. Maybe Meriam's your girl, but you don't *have* her—that I know. Come on, when did you really—"

"There was only one time," said Mark, hoarse and ashamed. "In the university, a foreign girl, from Nordica—I didn't even really like her, but—but the Saint girls are so prickly . . ."

"Do you like me?" said Helen calmly. She was unbuttoning her tunic.

"Yes, tremendously . . ."

Then Mark ran out of conversation, for Helen had pulled her tunic over her head, and sat bare from the navel up. She must have done a lot of swimming, for her tan was perfect all over. Her breasts were like ripe golden apples.

And at once her fingers were on his jacket, unbuttoning it. Next, she stripped off her own shorts.

Seconds later, Mark too was naked. And Helen pulled him down onto her on the bank.

For a timeless time there was joyous lust, without measure and without restraint. When it was over, and he lay back panting on the bank, the golden naked girl reached over and ruffled his hair.

"Mark, you're really nice." She laughed. "And only your second time! You're a fast learner. Poor boy—I hope I can do you good."

"You did me very good, my sweet, my sweet," said Mark, caressing her nipples.

Helen stroked him in return, running her fingers across his waist just above his navel.

"Mark, what's this scar you've got here, right across your middle?"

He laughed bitterly. "Don't you know? The Elders draw a knife across us there, when we reach the age of thirteen. It's the Holy Cut—the Holy Scar. It doesn't hurt much at the time, but it's a symbol—that we Saints have got to restrain our 'lower desires,' and only use them in the approved fashion, namely for breeding."

Helen shuddered. "How horrible! Poor boy. Do they do that to the girls as well?"

"Yes. Only, it's the *female* Elders who do it in *their* case. Meriam was very proud of her Scar."

He shook his head, stretched his naked limbs over the grassy bank, and surveyed the blue plain, the grazing herds. "I don't want to think of that now. Only of us, my darling." And his hands found Helen's shoulders.

She drew back slightly. "Darling? That's a word I'm not fond of. Mark, my sweet, don't exaggerate. I like you, yes, but I'm not sure . . . Anyway, you're going to marry Meriam some day."

"Blast Meriam. Who says I have to? I can always denounce the arrangement."

"Mark," said Helen, "we've only just begun to know each other. Now that you've had—now that we've both had what we've been so badly wanting, well, maybe you can begin to take me more calmly."

"Calmly? I'd like to take you *another* way."

He grabbed her, and he felt her laughingly submit. Again the glory rose in him. A native bird cried musically, high up in the golden sky.

And then suddenly the all-loving world was shattered. An enormous roar, a whinnying scream.

Mark scrambled to his feet. Helen, crouching naked, cried, "Mark! Our hexip!"

Back on the edge of the forest there was a flurry of animal limbs. The hexip was rearing, striking out with its hoofed toes. But it was hampered by its tether—its natural defense in any case was flight. Now it stood no chance against the six murderous paws of the huge blue-furred Dextran lion.

Mark dived for his discarded uniform trousers. He took several seconds to get the pistol out of its holster. Then he rushed toward the trees.

The hexip was down now, and the leoid was ravaging it. Mark gave the gun full power, and blasted off half the predator's neck and the back of its brain. The blue-gray form leaped convulsively, and fell back, a bleeding, lifeless mess.

The naked boy and girl knelt over their former steed.

"It's no good," said Helen, half tearful. "He's dead."

"Then we'd better get our clothes on," said Mark. "We've got a long walk ahead of us."

They were footsore when they opened the door in the Frontier fence and stepped into Classica. Mark was very thankful to see the other hexip standing tethered to the young pine. He felt he had had his bellyful of wild Dextran nature—enough to last him for quite a while. It was a relief to see humdrum green trees.

Helen had been very silent on the walk through the black-and-purple forest. Now as they waddle-cantered towards Sunion she hugged him tightly once, as they rode tandem, and said, "We're late for lunch—and I'm going to cop it. Never mind, Mark, it was worth it!" She paused, then whispered, "I *really* like you."

He felt awkwardly for her hand and pressed it. "I love you, Helen," he said.

Then they were reaching the stables—and there was the family: Julian, Jason, Helen's mother Clio, and a whole gaggle of faun servitors. Meriam stood in the background, close beside Sybil Lee.

When they had dismounted, Julian said, "We're glad to see you back, Master Turner. We found the Frontier key missing. My daughter has had strict orders never to go Outside without my permission. I suppose she didn't tell you that." He looked at their single hexip. "Helen, where's Bucephalus?"

"Dead," said the girl, and told the whole story, omitting only the details of what she and Mark had been doing on the edge of the blue plain when the leoid attacked. "Mark got the leo," she concluded. "It was real smart shooting."

"All right," said Julian coldly, and turned to Mark. "Do you wish to add anything to this account, Mark?"

"Only that I'm just as much to blame as Helen, Master Steader. I have funds, I'd like to reimburse you for the loss—"

"Be silent!" said Julian, his jaw twitching. "Sir, do not insult me! In Classica a host does not take money—" He checked himself. "Pardon me, Mark. You don't know our ways. I find no fault in you. But as for my daughter . . ." He swung around to face her. "You, wench, you will submit yourself to your punishment. If you were a year younger, I'd ask Clio to tan your hide. But as it is —since you have run so wild, wild you shall be deemed— till sunrise tomorrow." He nodded to his wife. "Take her away."

Mark tried to protest, but Helen said quietly, "It's all right, Mark. I had it coming. See you later."

Mark had a late lunch served to him in his bedroom. As Topsy was leaving, Meriam came in.

Mark looked at her guiltily. She looked as if she might have been weeping. But Meriam uttered no reproaches. She sat on the bed by him and clasped his shoulder.

"Oh Mark, I'm so glad you got back safely. They told me it wasn't really dangerous, but I couldn't help worrying." Her lip trembled. "Was—was she nice, after all?"

"Oh—all right," he said awkwardly, looking at the floor. "Do you understand—can you tell me what they are doing to her?"

"She's locked up in her room, without food. An old-fashioned punishment."

"No food! What, till tomorrow sunrise?"

"She'll be at dinner with us. Sybil says that's part of her punishment. I don't understand what that means. They're not bad people, but funny sometimes." She paused, then said more brightly, "Mark, are you going to do some work on those fauns this afternoon?"

"Suppose so."

"Then can I help you? I knew roughly what you were after, and the women helped me find the tallest and the shortest and some mothers with babies. They're waiting in the back yard."

"OK, Meriam," said Mark, rising. "Let's get on with it. Oh, and—thanks."

Dinner that evening was not a very enjoyable social occasion. Helen was there all right—but this time she was given a chair. Meriam's chair, for Meriam had submitted to Classican custom: she had discarded her sandals, tucked up her bare feet, and reclined on the couch next to Sybil.

Helen was pale and silent. As the first dishes were brought in, Mark noticed that none were being placed on Helen's table. Then Julian addressed his daughter.

"Well, my wood nymph, what will you have?"

"A golden apple," said Helen. "Only one, please."

And the boy-faun Gollibub brought in on a purple platter, and presented to Helen, a single pseudo-orange.

"But—but," said Mark. "That's *native* food!"

Jason Anders leered. "Sure is, son. And our Helen's gotta eat it. Every last bit."

"But they taste vile—like the worst sort of cough mixture."

"Just the medicine for wayward wenches," said Jason righteously.

Helen managed to eat her Golden Apple slowly, methodically, without flinching or retching. Mark ate very little himself that evening.

The thought struck him, as they retired, that this was just a touch of the *capital* punishment meted out by the Government of the Saints.

Helen would not starve, but by next morning she might be feeling pretty sick.

PART TWO:

The Voyage

Chapter Five

Mark had left the curtains of his windows undrawn, and the first light of Dextra's dawn woke him. He got up, shaved, bathed, and dressed, and then wandered over to the east window to watch the sunrise.

Of course, he did not actually see the disk of the Sun. With a sea-level air pressure of 1.8 Earth atmospheres, and multiple cloud layers to match, real blue sky was a monstrous rarity on Dextra. The planet's rotation period (23.6 standard hours) had been determined from space before the First Landing on the shores of Isthmia: Dextran astronomers would have had a hard time working it out exactly from the surface. What Mark now saw was a growing pale gold over the sea, throwing into sharp relief the coast of Classica, especially the dark bulk of Cape Sunion and the black pine woods above that cliff.

Soon, he thought, they will be releasing Helen from her captivity. Shall I go to her? I'd have to get past her family . . . Meriam . . .

Life was becoming complicated.

And then, gazing moodily out at the milky blue of Sunion Bay, he saw the ship. A seemingly tiny sailcraft, with pinkish canvas spread, making around the eastern cape toward the stead's harbor-jetty.

Could it be the Lee family boat, his one hope of transport to Anthis? Well, she was heading straight for that jetty.

There was a sharp rap on his door. It opened, and young Theseus Anders stood before him. The boy was dancing with excitement.

"Mark, you know what? Dymion's arrived! Just like Cynthia said. You coming?"

Everyone seemed to have trooped down to the jetty, including Helen, Meriam, and even a little group of blue-skinned faun servants. Dymion and his crew on the boat were already tying up.

When he saw the "crew," Mark forgot all about his love problems.

There were dozens of them—surely much more than were needed to handle the ropes or sail the ship. And they were fauns—more or less. The daylight was now quite strong, and colors were clear.

These fauns were nearly as naked-skinned as human men or women. Like human men or women they had a little tuft of pubic hair, and thick graceful locks falling from their scalps to about their shoulders. The males had some body fur, but only on their legs from mid-thigh downward, and that not much thicker than a somewhat hirsute man's. The females were quite bare-skinned, with small but shapely breasts. Both sexes had nipples, or pseudo-nipples, in the correct human places.

Mark had the impression that they were taller than the Sunion fauns. But, most striking difference of all, their naked skins were *green*, their body and head hair *blue*.

"Hey!" called Jason Anders, cupping his hands around his mouth. "You gotten us a new breed again, Dimmy?"

Endymion Lee came to the small ship's side. He was a

stockily built man of some thirty years, dark-faced, high-cheek-boned, shaggy with reddish-brown shoulder-length hair and an ample reddish beard. He was dressed in a red loincloth knotted sarong-wise at the waist, and a faded purple sea cloak slung over one shoulder. He was barefoot and bronzed wherever his skin was visible. Mark could see the resemblance to his sister Cynthia in his face; but the assurance of the way he stood suggested rather his mother Sybil.

Endymion jumped nimbly onto the jetty.

"Friends, family—and strangers," he said, casting a quick glance over the small crowd of welcomers, "what I have brought, I have brought. Anyway, there are forty of them, no less, and they all came out of the Anthis jungle begging and praying to be sold west. Hello, Mother—how are my Pyrrha and Pandora? Ah, there you are, my little dears." And immediately he was embracing his two small daughters, who had rushed forward into his arms, and ruffling their hair, and teasing them.

"Endymion," snapped Sybil, "where's your father?"

"Playing the fool in his own house—where should he be? Actually, he may equally well be in that jungle, for all I know—he spends enough time there. And, to cut short the catechism, here's a rundown on the rest of us: Rosina is keeping the stead together in her usual inimitable way—she sends you all her love, and she'll try to make it here on our next voyage. As for Kim, he's somewhere round Flora too. I didn't need him to crew on this trip; the fauns and little dryads reeved their ropes perfectly. Anyway, Kim's become too dreamy a natureboy these days to be much good as a sailor. You know how some people go over there."

Sybil said grimly, "I do indeed. Poor Kim! He too!"

"Who's Kim?" whispered Mark to Helen.

"Kimon—the youngest Lee brother. He's about my age.

Sybil wanted him to stay with us here too, but he wouldn't."

And now the new fauns were coming ashore. Yes, it was true: these were taller than the Sunion fauns, 140 centimeters and more—in fact, no longer the size of human children, but of small human adults, or half-grown teenagers. Mark stared. This close to, he saw their faces. They were definitely less goblinlike, more elvish. Their ears were still pointed, but shorter; their lips were fuller. The girl-fauns—

It didn't matter that they were green with blue hair. Some of them—most of them—they were pretty!

"My gods," said Clio Anders, staring. "Julian, if we keep *these,* they'll *have* to wear clothes!"

Endymion looked at her, and laughed.

"Yes, Rosina takes the same attitude at home. But that in itself leads to problems, my dear sister-in-law. Watch out for your men with your maids. See what I mean? They will to't, as the old bards used to say, unless you mean to geld and spay all the youth o' the stead."

Dymion had nodded in the direction of Jason Anders. Jason was already patting, or petting, one of the little green nympths, and Doris was expostulating with him.

"In the name of all that's decent," exploded Sybil, "my children, this has got to stop. Dymion, I don't know what demon is driving these creatures out of that eastern jungle —call her Hexate if you like, it doesn't matter—and it doesn't matter perhaps to the world at large if she has already bemused Lucius and debauched the rest of you at Flora; but I'm not having Classica overrun by these little green demi-devils. It can't go on! It can't go on!"

"But it can, Mother," said Dymion, "and it will. Calm yourself! What's happening needn't be anything very terrible or mysterious. My guess is this: there were many more species of fauns than we realized. We first came upon the less human-looking ones, the little gobblers, but now we are getting these that are bigger and—well—prettier. It's no good blaming me. If I retire from this business, some other enterprising Classican trader will take it up. I don't believe even thunders from the Saints or Navy skimmers will stop it. The fact is, your Classican way of life has come to depend to a large extent already on what amounts to slave labor. I am merely providing much improved slave labor, and if I don't, someone else will. It's the logic of history. You will end up with a society very like that of Earthly Greece or Rome or the American antebellum South; but with one enormous difference."

Dymion paused for rhetorical effect: but Meriam spoiled his effect by cutting in:

"I know what that difference will be. You can't possibly have any miscegenation. Or any manumission, if you Classican steaders have your way, and brand these poor things as animals. But just wait till we take up this matter with General Control!"

Dymion looked deflated. "Oh," he said. "And who may you be, my Mistress-in-Green-Trousers?"

"Meriam Turner, sociologist, on vacation-study from the University of New Jerusalem. And this is my cousin Mark Turner, zoologist—"

"Look," said Mark urgently, "Master Lee, you say these fauns stepped out of the forest and *asked* to be sold? Why did they ask? And in what language?"

Dymion sighed. "Let's take that first question first. Why are these slaves so eager to be shipped? Well, I don't know. Perhaps they're being driven by population pressure, or the spirit of adventure, or something. Certainly our bit of Anthis is teeming with fauns. As to what language—why, English of course. What other language is current on this planet? The fauns are picking it up from each other. We have lit a candle, you know, in our stead of Flora, teaching our house-fauns to speak, and it's turning into a bonfire. They're fantastically quick learners.

Articulate speech is spreading right across the continent, wherever there is any kind of faun or gobbler. Just think of that! Is it not a sublime conception? From the plains of Centauria in the north to the steaming jungles of Hind in the south, the whisper spreads, the immortal spark, the *logos!* Sometimes, when I hold forth to those earnest green-and-blue jungle folk, I feel like a god, like Thoth, Prometheus, and Michelangelo's finger-pointing Jehovah rolled into one! They're avid, those wood sprites, I can tell you—they love memorizing words, proverbs, jingles, anything: I feel sorely tempted to teach them *Paradise Lost* and Shakespeare's sonnets and my own latest masterpieces . . ."

"All right, Dymion, that's enough," said Julian Anders wearily. "Once you get going with your nonsense there's no stopping you, and we've none of us had our breakfasts yet. Can you get those new fauns of yours back onto your boat for the time being? I don't want them disorganizing our current staff. Then we humans can discuss matters over rolls and coffee, up at the house."

Endymion turned to his swarming green crew, and made a large shooing gesture.

"Once more into the ship, dear friends, once more . . ." he began.

As they were trooping docilely back into the craft, Mark touched Dymion on the shoulder.

"Could you lend me a couple? Preferably a male and a female. I'm studying fauns for a doctoral thesis, and I'd like to compare this breed with the others."

Dymion regarded him for a moment in silence, then grinned.

"Well, well—chalk up another success for the old family witchcraft. My father prophesied that I would meet someone across the sea who would show great interest in the *fauna* of Flora. He also requested me to encourage him. With such credentials, Master Turner, how can I refuse?

Halloo there, my merry men all! Fufluns, Florimel, will you two step ashore a minute?"

Soon the two green fauns stood before Mark, eyeing him with an air of friendly interest.

"At your service, Maister," said Fufluns, bowing. "Will ye be native unto these shores, or outlandish?"

"I'faith, 'a has an uncouth look," suggested Florimel, "what wi' his strange garments, his trews and buskins."

"Now, now, you two," frowned Dymion, "that's enough. You are here not to inspect, but be inspected." He turned to Mark. "You see what I mean about their logophilia? You'll find this breed fluent, but as for the brand of English—well, I apologize in advance for what you'll have to put up with. I'm afraid I indulged a few of my whims there . . . and besides, I happened to have some old play texts with me in Flora, nice colloquial stuff for reading aloud, and they lapped it up."

Trading arrangements were quickly settled up at the stead-house. Dymion sold nearly all his green-skinned fauns to the Anders brothers, in return for certain stores plus a moderate credit with the Bank of Eirenis. Details were being finalized when the family and guests gathered for lunch.

"I'm keeping back a couple of my crew," explained Dymion when he had drained his first cup of Classican wine. "Huon and Hylo I need to help sail the *Naiad* back to Anthis. Of course, I might just make do with the blue fellows I'm taking back with me in exchange, but they're a bit small, say, for helmsmen."

"What blue fellows? What exchange?" asked Clio.

"Your menfolk are giving me eight of those," said Dymion, nodding to the small waiters. "Four boys, four girls. They were my crewmates coming here last year. You can spare them. Besides," he added, swallowing a grape, "those little fellows made me a deputation this morning. Gollibub, Springol, Topsy and so on—they want to come back."

"What?" said Sybil sharply. "I never heard anything like *that* before."

"Nor did I," said Dymion, "but you must remember, Mother, till last year there were only common gobblers, full-hairies, waiting to welcome me on the shores of Classica—and they were, well, not overbright. Maybe it shows increasing intelligence in our fauns, that some of them are getting homesick. Anyhow, you won't miss eight half-hairy fauns! With my new lot, you'll be overstocked as it is."

"Not for long, we won't," said Jason. "Once we've trained the greenskins we'll sell off all the others, west along the Coast, and clear a handsome profit." He pondered. "Hey, Dimmy, d'you think we can train our fauns to *lie?*"

"With whom? Sorry, Mother. All right, I'll be serious. What lies did you have in mind, Jason?"

"Before we sell 'em, I'd like them to learn a story for the buyers in the West. I'd like 'em to say they're native-born and bred in Sunion. Result of our own breeding methods. That way, maybe we can keep a monopoly on this Eastern sea trade for a while longer."

"Ah," said Dymion. "I see, Jason, you're on the trail of another fast golden fleece. Well, it's worth trying. Fauns, as I said before, are eager learners. Whether they're given to lying—that's a big question. I wish I knew the answer to that myself." He tossed back his head and drained his wine. "Another and another cup to drown . . ."

"Er—excuse me," said Mark diffidently. Dymion was putting away the wine remarkably quickly: Mark wanted to catch him before the midday heat and the meal and the alcohol made him drowsy. "Master Lee, thank you for lending me those—er—specimens; I got very interesting data from them. But now I have another favor to ask.

Would you—would you have room on your boat for passengers?"

"Ship," said Dymion, putting down his emtpy cup and reaching for the replenishing jar. "Ship, scaphos, nau, caravel, galiot, argosy—not boat! The *Naiad* sails like a dream, has cabins fit for princes—or princesses." He smiled. "Don't worry, young man, Julian has put your problem to me already, and I'm willing. It will be a pleasure to have new human faces around Flora after so long. Yes, I hereby invite you both to be our guests at Flora for as long as the fancy takes you. You see, I include in the deal your Green-Trouser Princess—in fact, now that I've seen her, I wouldn't sail without her." He laughed across the room at Meriam, who had reverted to her uniform since Dymion's arrival, and was sitting up straight in her chair. "Ha, me proud beauty," continued Dymion, raising his cup in a mock toast, "I shall carry you off, Puss-in-Boots, boots and all."

"And me," said Helen quietly. "Without boots, of course."

Helen's remark caused something of a sensation—in fact, a small family row. But Dymion and his sister Cynthia, and Helen's mother Clio, all took the girl's side.

"Let her go," said Clio wearily. "She's been a nuisance here for months—I've been expecting her to run off every time a salesman came by in his boat, or when we've gone shopping to the nearest town. At least in Flora there's a very limited number of men she can sleep with, and they're all at least half decent, not strangers, yet not immediate family. It's the end of the human world there, and if she doesn't get eaten by absent-minded native monsters, she can't come to much harm."

"No?" said Sybil. "Clio—"

"Oh, spare me the bogies, Sybil," said Clio. "I don't believe in them. You Lees are all half witches and mystery-mongers, but what's there to be afraid of? I know what *you* mean by depravity, Sybil; but I reckon we're going to get that here, anyway, with these handsome new fauns. I don't think I mind that nearly so much as—well—*incest.*"

After that there was a tense silence. It was broken by Dymion. He yawned.

"I guess I'll take a nap now, and see to my *Naiad* this evening. I'm needed back at Flora as soon as possible. I'd like to sail at dawn tomorrow."

The men and womenfolk of Sunion were busy that afternoon and evening finding quarters for the new fauns, and arranging to feed them. Helen was fully occupied in this work—her mother kept her at it—and Meriam was an interested observer. Mark looked on too for a while, then retired to his room to work on his zoological notes.

He contemplated a table:

Genus *Satyrus*

Species	*Date of Discovery* (D.E.)	*Average Height* (cm)	*Brain Capacity* (cc)
tetradactylus ("tailed gobbler")	316	100	400
erectus ("common gobbler")	422	117	600
seminudus* ("blueskin")	513	133	800**
viridis* ("greenskin")	514	142	1000**

*Provisional name. **Rough estimate.

There were some things about this table which made him uneasy. It looked like a straight evolutionary series. And indeed from all the physical evidence he'd gathered, each new species of *Satyrus* could be the direct descendant of the previous one. The height increase seemed to be leveling off. That was natural, for there would be a maximum size for an efficient Dextran biped, and the fauns were now approaching that. But the brain capacity was *not* leveling off. And the interval between discoveries was shortening dramatically. . . .

More curious facts:

The newest fauns, the greenskins, had no estrus cycle. According to their own testimony, their green girls were "always beautiful, ever fair."

They, too, claimed that "the forest was their mother." And they knew of no smaller fauns in Anthis—not even, now, any *blue*skins. . . .

Their intelligence level, Mark guessed, was quite close to that of *Homo sapiens*. They were voluble in their queer English. And yet there was a fey *otherness* about them; perhaps a secretiveness.

Like the blueskins, they too showed an extremely small variation in height—no more than 6 centimeters.

And again like the blueskins, the nipples of the females were quite nonfunctional.

"Why, they're just given us for beauty spots, Maister," Florimel had said brightly.

At dinner that night Meriam wore her uniform again, but no shoes, and reclined between Sybil and Cynthia. She looked tired; during the meal, she talked in low tones mostly to Cynthia. Helen, reclining next to her mother, looked ravishing in her loose Classican dinner gown, and Mark determined to ravish her at the next opportunity she gave him. He thought her conversation sparkling, too. It appeared that she very much liked the new fauns.

"How very nice that we'll have two of them on the *Naiad* with us," she said.

Dymion drained his wine cup, and gave both young girls an impartial leer.

"One for each of you," he said.

Finally, the dinner was over. Mark pleaded sleepiness and went promptly to his room. And waited.

Well, he thought, Meriam would be here by now if she intended to protect my virtue. So . . .

He undressed, and turned off the light, and waited, tingling with the expectation of that utter bliss.

By the time three moons had risen, three dim cloudy haloes glimmering through his east window, he realized the bitter truth. No one was coming to his bed that night.

Oh hell, he thought, maybe her mother has locked her up again. Well, there's always that ship. . . .

Chapter Six

The little ship stood out on milky Tethys, moving with a fair breeze, riding gently in rhythm with the slow swell. Several kilometers behind, Sunion was already blurring into the gray-green coastline of Classica.

The four humans stood on the poop deck, leaning against the stern rail, making the most of the freshness of the breeze. Ahead, the big purple fore-and-aft sail billowed tautly beyond the figure of the green faun Hylo, who held the helm, steering a steady easterly course.

The *Naiad*, Dymion had explained, was basically a *scapho*—a single-masted ship of a type once common on the Greek seas of old Earth. There were two large sails, one on the forestay and one running back from the mast along a rope like a curtain rail to the point of a huge angled sprit. This big mainsail could be spread or furled very quickly by tugging on a pulley—just as a window curtain can be drawn by pulling on a vertical cord. In fact, the whole rigging was designed for easy, quick handling by a tiny crew, and of course nobody had to go aloft. The materials which made up the ship were primitive, but fairly efficient. For instance, the mast and sprit were cut stems of tubolia—an unusually slim-trunked tree, native in Anthis, partly hollow inside like bamboo, but very strong for its weight, like the bones of a bird.

There was a low covered cargo deck running the length of the vessel, some 16 meters, and at the stern there was a handsome two-roomed raised cabin under the poop. The cabin and poop structures were all carved with dolphins and picked out in gold and purple paint.

Dymion smiled, looking at the carved wood dolphins. "All my own work," he said. "At least, literally: we swiped the design for the whole of these sternworks from a picture of a Dutch yacht, Earthly seventeenth century—my favorite period for art as well as poetry. Nice, isn't it?"

The girls stood on either side of Mark, Helen in her short tunic, Meriam in her green uniform.

"Beautiful," said Meriam. "Dymion, where do we sleep?"

They had left their luggage on the main deck, without inspecting the cabins. But already Mark foresaw certain problems.

"No great problem," said Dymion, grinning. "Look at the fauns." The little blueskins were scampering about forward, on the main deck. "There's ample room in the cargo hold, down below there, and we're a fairly empty ship. On the other hand, if you want to travel in style, come down and look at the cabin quarters."

They went down the wooden ladder. There were two rather bare cabins, one right at the stern, the other just forward of that. The stern cabin was fitted with bookshelves and a chart table. Neither cabin had bunks.

"I prefer mattresses," said Dymion. "You'll find them stowed in those wall lockers when you want them."

"Yes," said Meriam, "but which of these is the women's cabin?"

Dymion raised his eyebrows. "As skipper, I sleep in the stern one—so as to nip up that ladder when necessary and take over the helm or shout orders to my faithful crew, and so on. For the rest of you—well, mattresses are flexible, aren't they? That's one of their great virtues. You can sleep where and with whom you please."

Meriam turned pink, but said evenly, "I know what you mean, Master Lee, but that's not our Livyan custom. If—if Helen and Mark want to share a cabin, I'll not stand in their way; but I won't share yours. If it's fine, I could sleep on deck. Otherwise, as you say, there's the cargo hold."

"That's my Saintly girl," said Dymion, grinning delightedly. "You'll be sleeping with the fauns there—with Gollibub and Bruny and Springol and Rutter and those lovely big green boys when they're off duty. They've only got four females between the six of them, so you should certainly get your share of attention. I don't think Mopsa and Topsy will be jealous."

Suddenly Mark had had enough of Dymion's brand of humor. "Meri," he said, "please, there's no problem. I'm not going to share a cabin with Helen." He turned to Dymion. "I think it would be reasonable for the two girls to share—well, the forward cabin. *I* can sleep anywhere else."

Dymion shrugged. "All right—be my messmate, Mark. At least to start with. Lord, we know what we are, but we know not what we may be. . . ."

When they had stowed their luggage, Mark got out his diary and checked the date: Friday, June 31. What, only three days out of Livya? Yes—but already he felt like a traveler through three new worlds. Classica, the purple world beyond Classica, and now the strange little world of this ship.

He was worried for a while about Dymion: he felt there would be trouble in store if he kept on needling Meriam. Meri, after all, was a girl of some spirit, and she wouldn't stand for it; no more should she. And, if it came to that, he couldn't stand for it himself: Meri was his cousin, and under his protection.

But in fact, after the accommodation question was settled, Dymion quieted down. He dropped his rather forced gallantry, his aggressive ungallantry, and his would-be pregnant quotations, and became almost considerate to all his young passengers.

Around noon on the first day he spread out a chart in the rear cabin, while the others clustered around.

"We're about here, I guess," he said, pointing. "Halfway across the Narrows. What some clown in the first century tried to label the New Bosporus, though the 'strait' is 180 kilometers wide. Tomorrow we should be abreast of New Asia—the north shore of the Midbar Desert. And, if the wind holds, the day after that we could be off the extreme west of Anthis—the flowery, the lush country." He straightened up. "I'll be happy when we see the shore on our right—then we can coast the rest of the way to Flora. Frankly, when we're out of sight of land, I can only guess where we are."

Meriam looked appalled. "Don't you have any navigational instruments? Gyros? Radar?"

"Hades, no," laughed Dymion. "That's not the way of things in my family. Gyros etcetera would cost us a packet, and to earn that packet we'd have to knuckle down to serious work—tie in with the whole damn civilized thing, maybe even pay taxes."

"Don't you do *that,* even, in Anthis?" said Mark. "The government—"

"There's no effective human government outside Livya and New Europe. You can thank the tidy minds in GenCon for that! Here be Provinces, here be tigroids . . . but those guys in New Jay have forgotten the mavericks, people like us Lees, who are willing to wander with a boat and a few sacks of seeds to unauthorized shores. Oh, I suppose it can't last—already there's talk, I believe, of declaring Anthis a Territory, and setting up permanent scientific stations, and then the tax man cometh. But till then—why, we mean to enjoy our anarchy while we can. It was my father who urged us to go to Flora; and I don't regret going along with him. With that stead, with this ship, I live like a prince. As to navigation —I can navigate pretty well with compass and log line; and maybe one day, when your government clamps down on Anthis, I'll pack my family into the *Naiad* and move on—elsewhere." He smiled. "My wife Rosina would like us to move back to Classica, but I think it might be fun to sail clean out of Tethys, over the Ocean to Hind or Kataya."

Mark and Meriam exchanged glances. "You *must* be joking," said Meriam. "There's nothing on the Southern Ocean or the eastern shore of the continent but purple life and native animals."

"There's not much else in Anthis," said Dymion, "just a few green vegetables around Flora. But we manage."

"No fence?" said Meriam suddenly.

"You guessed it, Greensleeves. And there wasn't at Sunion when we held the place. No need—really no need. As long as you keep your native livestock properly penned—your paracans and your hexips and so on—there's nothing much to worry about. That's a point few people seem to realize. Those purple jungles are *safer* for us humans than a green jungle would be, say on old Earth. Here on Dextra, we're inedible."

"But that cuts both ways," said Helen, frowning. "We

can't live off the land. I wouldn't mind being edible if I could eat, say, Golden Apples, and like them."

"Let's go up on deck," said Dymion, rolling up the map. "It's getting hot."

It was, too. On the poop, the breeze was a relief. Dymion exchanged a cheerful word with Huon, the green faun who was steering now, and then they all sprawled against the stern rail.

Helen shut her eyes against the cruel sky glare; Mark and Meriam gazed down at the milky blue sea. There was now no land in sight. In theory, Dextra's horizon would be farther off than a horizon on Earth, since the planet was bigger; but with the thicker atmosphere, it was rare to see the horizon line clearly at all. And one couldn't now: the world seemed to consist of a milky surface, then golden haze turning gradually into golden cloud towards the zenith.

"I wish," said Meriam after a while, "I wish the Lord had given us a planet where we could see *out*."

Mark was startled: he had never, ever heard Meriam question the ways of the Lord before. He said, "See out? See what?"

"Space. The sun. The moons, the stars. See old Sol, perhaps." She paused. "I wonder why we've never heard anything from there—from Earth, or Moon Base."

"Perhaps they blew it up," suggested Dymion, "just after the First Hundred left in their starship. Blew up the Moon colonies, I mean—they'd done for Earth already. They were still divided into national settlements even *there,* you know. Our ancestors came from Apollo City, the base of the so-called *Americans*. There were also the Russians and the Chinese, and each group was still hating the others even in those shut-in bubble cities. It's lucky there were enough likely planets to go around, among the nearer stars, when they launched the starships. Otherwise we might have had a three-way national war *here,* in our first century." He yawned. "That was a thoroughly nasty period—the end of Solar history. I prefer the earlier, more cultured centuries on Earth. Our ancestors did right to forget about Moon Base and all that. Why did you bring that up, Meri?"

"Well—it might be nice to hear from other humans, wouldn't it? Less lonely."

Dymion exchanged glances with Helen. Dymion shrugged; Helen said, "There's some of us who *don't* feel lonely on this planet, Meriam—not even in the purple wilds. *I* don't, for one; neither do the Lee family. 'Specially not the Lees."

Dymion got to his feet. "Dammit, it's getting as hot here as below. Time for lunch, anyway. Let's get it."

Dymion did not drink wine that midday—in fact, though he had a goodly supply of assorted jars and wineskins aboard, he took no more than a single cup of an evening for as long as they were at sea. Mark was pleased and surprised to realize that his "wildness," his rather flaunted character as the drunken poet, was only one side of his nature, and partly a pose at that. There was a streak of responsibility in Dymion. From what the Anders men had said in Sunion, Mark gathered that he was a shrewd bargainer; and now he turned out to be a good skipper as well.

"Must keep a steady head while we're sailing," he admitted that afternoon, almost apologetically. "There's only me and Hylo and Huon, basically, to keep us right side up."

"Can't we remedy that?" said Meriam earnestly, looking around at Mark and Helen. "After all, *we* are stronger than little fauns—you could teach us the ropes. When there's work going, it's Livyan custom to share it."

"Yes," said Mark, looking at the slight figure of Hylo at

the wheel. "Those two seem to have a heavy duty. Maybe you could show me how to manage that helm."

"I'll show you everything, you landlubbers," grinned Dymion. "You've asked for it, and you're going to get it. Consider yourselves under my orders, sailor boy and girls. First order: Willing-if-not-Able Seaman Meriam, you will at once strip those boots and socks off those pretty little feet of yours. Sailors must go barefoot. It helps your grip on the deck."

Meriam obeyed meekly and at once.

"My, what pretty ankles," said Dymion. "Greenpants, you're the nicest-looking sailor I've ever commanded."

To Mark's astonishment, Meriam looked pleased. She merely said with mock severity, "Really, Dymion, you ought to be ashamed at yourself! And you with a wife waiting for you in Flora!"

"Ah yes, my long-suffering Rosina," said Dymion with an exaggerated sigh. "But that cat's away now, you know. Come on, let's show you the ropes."

It now appeared that Helen did not need much teaching: she had "messed about" on Dymion's deck before, on his last visit to Sunion. For Mark and Meriam, the learning was fascinating, but sometimes tough going—they blistered their unhardened hands on the ropes, and occasionally tripped over the tackle on the deck. Once Meriam even tripped over Dymion, as the ship swayed and threw her upon him. Dymion did not let go of her quickly—certainly not quick enough for Mark's liking.

"You've got a good strong build for a girl, Meri," said Dymion appreciatively, allowing his hands to run over her hips as he righted her again. "Pity they don't allow bigamy any more. But who cares about formalities like that? 'Once aboard the lugger,' goes the old song, and you *are* aboard the lugger now—only it's a scapho."

Meriam moved away, but not too quickly. Dammit, thought Mark, does she have to look so coy?

By sunset they had all learned the basic skills, and Mark had even more or less mastered the art of helmsmanship: under his hands the *Naiad* did rather tend to swim sideways at first, but after a while he could cut down the yawing to a minimum, and he volunteered for a spell of real steering.

"For this relief much thanks," said Hylo coolly, and strolled forward to meet up with Huon. The greenskins mostly kept a bit apart from the little blue fauns, who appeared to regard their taller brothers with some awe. Now Helen emerged from the girl's cabin and went forward and joined the two bigger fauns. Mark saw that she was soon laughing with them, and putting her hands on their green shoulders.

An awful zoological query crossed his mind. Could they? Would they? There was no way of telling—yet. Perhaps Dymion would know.

And where the hell *was* Dymion? Where, for that matter, was Meriam? Both seemed to be in the cabins below; and it was now getting dark.

He was extremely glad when Huon relieved him at the wheel.

"How do you like Mistress Helen?" said Mark darkly. Helen and Hylo were still leaning over the forward rail.

"Faith, maister," said Huon, " 'tis a lass unparalleled —for a human."

As evening deepened into night, Mark felt better. There were no electric lights aboard the *Naiad,* and the primitive lanterns combined with the pale glow of the sea and the dim haloes of a couple of moons bathed the decks in a soft, pearly radiance. It was reasonably cool, and the ship was moving smoothly, sliding ever eastward. Helen had rejoined the humans, and all four of them had a simple dinner on the poop deck.

Earlier, when he had gone below, Mark had found

Meriam and Dymion together in the stern cabin, but sitting apart from each other, each reading a book drawn from Dymion's small shipboard library. Now he asked Meriam what book had so interested her.

She said hesitantly, "It was a very strange book—one that Cynthia had quoted to me. It was a kind of Scripture—but not any I'd ever heard of before! It's not even in the Discarded Apocrypha of the Saints—but maybe it ought to be. By an old Earth prophet—"

"Name of William Blake," said Dymion. "*I* taught Cynthia some of that. Picked up that copy in a second-hand shop on the Gibraltar Canal—it's precious. By the way, Meri, which line did Cynthia quote to you?"

"I—I can't say," said Meriam.

"No? Then I can guess," said Dymion. "I'm the least gifted of the Lees as regards the old family witchcraft, but, Meri, I can mind-hear you now, loud and clear. Was it 'the lust of the goat is the bounty of God'?"

"No," said Meriam faintly.

"No, it wasn't either. It was even better: 'The nakedness of woman is the work of God.' Amen to that, too." Did you get on well with my sister Cynthia, Meri?"

"Yes," said Meriam. "Please, I'm tired now, I think I'd like to sleep."

Helen declared that she was sleepy also.

"OK, let's all make an early night of it," said Dymion.

In the stern cabin, as he lay on his mattress, Mark could hear the two girls talking together in low tones. "Dymion," he said.

"What is it, shipmate?"

Mark put his zoological query.

Dymion laughed softly. "Who's to say? I haven't known this breed more than a few months, and in all that time at Flora there's only been my dear Rosina. And she, let me tell you, is a lady. They've been perfectly tame with her. But when it comes to a gal like Helen . . ."

"Do you know Helen well?"

"What do you think?" said Dymion. "I was there last year, remember, and she was all of fifteen."

Chapter Seven

The next day, June 32, the weather turned blustery, with thunderous clouds low over the sea bringing rain squalls. The humans and the two bigger fauns were kept busy till evening continually shifting sails and wrestling with the helm. Mark was nearly seasick once, but that passed: everyone else seemed to be all right. Helen was very gay, scampering about the deck: she seemed to enjoy helping the fauns haul on the ropes. Meriam was turning out to be a good, efficient sailor: she made little fuss, but she was thorough. She could manage the helm well, even in this difficult weather. The wind whipped at her dark hair, but she had that well secured in a tight, swept-back style. With her bare feet firmly planted on the heaving deck, and her capable hands gripping the wheel, she looked very much the typical Livyan sabra.

In fact, thought Mark, she looks almost pretty.

Toward evening the weather improved. They had run a good distance in the strong winds, and land was in sight on the starboard bow—the northern edge of the great Midbar desert, that desert which ran down the western flank of New Asia, barring off the settled human lands from the lush jungles farther east. As they took their supper on the poop, Dymion said, "Now, you know, we're entering a new world. New Asia . . . the gorgeous East. Well, it's not quite like the East of Old Earth. No great temples, no kings barbaric, no dancing girls, no gold. But dancing nymphs we have, and black jungles, and enormous lushness; and maybe the kings will come into their own, someday. A great and splendid civilization, with fauns for rajas and centaurs for courtiers—"

"Centaurs?" said Helen. "What d'you mean, Dymion?"

"Oh—oh, nothing," said Dymion hastily. "A rhetorical flourish—do I have to show my poetic license for it? But what I'm talking about is not nonsense. We are living in the infancy of a world. Dextra was maybe a sleeping princess—we humans are kissing her awake. Fertilizing her—making her pregnant with intelligence. After all, for all we know there was *no* intelligent species on Dextra when we first landed, and now there is. Like the sperm in the egg—if you'll forgive me, Meriam."

"I'm not a child," said Meriam. "I know what fertilization means. And it is a good thing—a glory. We must increase and multiply. If we can help Dextran life to increase and multiply too, why then, so much the greater glory."

Mark stared. "Meriam, you've changed," he said. "That's not orthodox!"

"No?" said Meriam. "But there are texts for it. 'For those that fear the Lord there are *two* Gardens—which of your Lord's blessings would you deny?' "

"If I may recall the Midrash—" said Mark drily. "But I won't tease you, Meri, because I feel the same way. That's the Atlantis way, incidentally."

"What's it really like," said Meriam wistfully, "in Atlantis?"

Mark pondered. "No—you never did ask me before, did you? Well—I loved Atlantis. Maybe I'm prejudiced—it's my native country, and I haven't seen it in nine years, and I suppose the population is much more already. But still. It's a lovely island, far enough out in the Western Ocean to have a mild climate, not far enough out to be out of touch with New Europe. There are blue hills as well as green hills, and small rivers and white cliffs, and the paracan lies down with the Earth dog, and there aren't too many Saints—nor any great sinners, for that matter. It's where I'd like to live, one day, when I've got my D.V."

"Your what?" said Helen.

"Doctor Veritatis—a degree, Doctor of Truth. It's easier to get in zoology than in some other subjects, bcause the Truth as defined by the Saints tends to get a little twisted—say, in sociology." He waited for Meriam to attack him, but she said nothing, so he continued. "Well, I need that degree to eat. But there are other labs and universities besides New Jay—smaller ones, where maybe they don't pay you so well, but enough. Like Westron, Atlantis. Westron's a little town, not much bigger than your Eirenis. It's got green gardens, and it's surrounded by blue hills and green-and-purple woods."

"No leoids?" said Helen.

"No. The Appleseeders didn't even have to kill them off—they just hadn't reached the island."

"Or maybe St. Patrick charmed them away," murmured Dymion. "Well, Mark, you'll find New Asia a bit like your Atlantis—but much, much lusher."

By the morning of the 33rd and last day of June they were only a kilometer off the New Asian coast, and the shore was turning from tawny yellow to the blue of native grass.

"The end of the desert," said Dymion, "and we should make Port Nysa by evening. That's a little bay, quite a sheltered harbor. What do you say we spend a night ashore there? We're making good time; we can afford to stretch our legs."

"Oh yes, let's!" said Helen.

"Besides," said Dymion, smiling, "it's Midsummer Eve. That used to be a famous festival on Old Earth. I suggest we ought to celebrate. Break out the wine."

"What's at Nysa?" said Meriam. "Is there a stead?"

"Oh no. Just a hut that was left there by an exploring party a couple of years back. But it's a pleasant spot—*nicer* than most along this coast." He laughed. "I guess that's how it got its name."

They anchored the *Naiad* securely fifty meters out, and left her in the care of Huon and the two blue faun maids, Topsy and Mopsa. Then everyone else piled into the ship's boat, and Hylo and Dymion slowly rowed them ashore.

It was good to feel solid ground underfoot again. But this was the ground of a new country—Anthis, New Asia. It was already twilight, and one could just make out the flitting sparks of fireflies in the black trees beyond the beach. There was again that thrilling bittersweet smell of native Dextra—but seemingly both more bitter and more sweet at once, more intense altogether, than the smell of New Europe beyond the Frontier of Classica. Here and there, Mark could see the paleness of huge flowers.

The evening clouds had thinned to pure cirrus. All four moons were up, their tiny haloes constellated in the eastern sky, over the forest. From out of the darkness of the forest came a stream, clear fresh water cutting through the beach and into the sea, with a faint ripple over pebbles. And near the bank of the stream stood the half-ruined hut.

The little blue fauns were excited. The source of their excitement was not so much the sense of the land, for this was not yet their own native country: the two females, Lucy and Lulu, had just come into heat; rather to

Meriam's embarrassment and Helen's amusement, for everyone had been at close quarters in the boat.

"We'll have mercy on them," said Dymion. "Have them dump all our stores here, in front of this hut; then give them a skin of native wine, and let them make merry on their own, in the bushes. Hylo, my faithful Faun Friday, you shall help us get a fire going, and then you can join your little blue brothers—at least to the extent of sharing their wine. I don't suppose the other thing would interest you, with those."

"No indeed, good Maister," said Hylo, "for we are spirits of another sort—of nobler shape, erect and tall. I'll bring thee in wood, I'll show thee all the qualities o'the isle—"

"You're getting your texts mixed," said Dymion coldly. "Anyhow, this isn't an isle. Fetch us in fuel, hag-seed, and be quick about it."

The fauns were all away now, and the fire was glowing. By its light, they ate and drank.

"To us—to Nysa—to Midsummer—to the fauns, bless their little hearts," said Dymion, raising his wine cup. "Let copulation thrive. Meri, my dear, you are looking ravishing tonight."

Meriam had certainly surprised everybody, Mark thought. She must have been given a farewell present by the ladies of Sunion; for now she was wearing it—a loose Classican gown caught up at one shoulder by an aluminum brooch. Her other shoulder and both arms were quite bare, except for aluminum bracelets that jingled and glittered quite paganly. In fact, the only difference between her garb and Helen's was that Meri had worn her loose-fitting Classican sandals, whereas Helen was barefoot as always.

In the firelight, reclining beside Dymion, Meriam looked utterly different from the prickly Livyan sabra Mark had known. His boring, virginal, impossible girl-cousin—what had come over her? He didn't know, or he didn't like to think.

"Meri," he said at last, after the wine had circulated several times, "are you wearing *anything* under that glorified sheet?"

Helen pressed herself against Mark and laughed. "I know what she's wearing—I saw her put it on. No secrets among us girls! A waist-cloth—that's what. That's the correct Classican ladies' underwear for a dinner robe. So am I wearing a waist-cloth, Mark—not shorts. I'm a lady for once. D'you like that?"

"Yes—yes—"

"Stop flirting, you two," said Dymion, "and pass the wine back this way."

Mark didn't quite like the way the conversation was going. He changed the subject.

"Dimmy, I've been meaning to ask you a question. Who—or what—is Hexate?"

" 'Who is Silvia, what is she-ee,' " sang Dymion. "Come on Mark—have a guess. What does the word suggest?"

"Well, the nearest moon is called Hecate—"

"Right. And Hecate was an old Earth goddess, a witch-goddess—our lowest moon is named for her. How about the syllable 'hex'?"

"Six?"

"Good boy. Go to the top of the class. I think that's what was in my father's mind—a six-limbed witch-goddess. Only I can't be quite sure, because you see he dreamed her."

"Dreamed?"

"It's a bad habit some of us have, you know—dreaming. We're much given to it in the Lee family. Not my mother, not my wife Rosina—but they're only Lees by marriage. The true Lee line can be traced back to a Chinese-American physicist named Li—spelt L,I—one of the

First Hundred. Well, officially he was a physicist. Our family tradition has it that he was also a wizard—at least, powerfully endowed with that gift of ESP that's now been proscribed as heresy in New Jerusalem. Alister Li was an expert on Tarot and I Ching and other methods of divination—anyhow, he injected a much-needed element of superstition into the simon-pure scientific society of the First Hundred. Whence, us. Well, to get back to Hexate—my father simply dreamed her, seven years ago in Sunion, and he drew her on paper the next morning. I carved her in stone from his drawing. He said he saw her just like that in a forest with the dawn rising over the trees. That's all I can tell you."

"But you think it's significant?"

"Of course. Dreams like that, clear vivid dreams—they always are. It was Hexate, really, who led my father to emigrate to our eastern forest of Flora. But what Hexate signifies, exactly, we've yet to find out." Dymion yawned. "Mark, this conversation has been getting too serious. Let's open another wine jar. I have a rather special one here—I'm sure you'll like it."

"Not for me," said Meriam. "I've had enough already, Dimmy."

Dimmy, indeed! thought Mark. What's she playing at, my affianced bride? Oh, well, to hell with her!

He held out his wine cup, and so did Helen, and the three of them drank from the new jar.

It was a bitter wine, bitter, dark, and potent. You got used to the taste after a while, the effects were so marvelous. The fire had died down, but the fireflies were very bright, and the moons were almost piercing the clouds. Lights were burgeoning everywhere, and faun laughter rang in the woods. Mark felt liberated, godlike.

"Tastes like hell," he said thickly, through the reeling confusion. "Still, *Dimmy*—"

"C'mon, c'mon," said a girl's voice, "never mind Dimmy . . ."

There was a hand on his arm, and the whirling got worse. Dextra was moving under him—no, he was moving over Dextra. Best way to move over Dextra—fly. Sprout midlimb wings. Be a bat-monkey. The fauns were really bat-monkeys. Be a faun, then.

His head cleared a little: now they were among the trees. How had they got there? Never mind. The girl was against him, under him, she was Dextra opening her thighs, naked flesh, naked native, navel to navel, glory expanding . . .

There were unhuman squeals in the bushes, squeals close by. The fauns and their girls were playing too.

And then it was over, and his head cleared still more, and he was lying on her. Lying on Helen's naked body, with a firefly flitting past his face.

"What—" he began.

"Mark, that was lovely," said Helen's voice. "I'm sorry I've been a bitch to you. We must do it more often."

There was a coldness on his right foot. The stream: his toes were in the stream.

He did not even wonder how he came to be naked.

"Let's have a bathe," said Helen.

They were both in the stream, splashing each other, laughing among the reeds. And then suddenly he heard a cry from the direction of the beach.

"Mark, Mark—"

He tensed, whirled about. The cry came again. Then he knew, and the knowledge chilled him sober. It was Meriam. Calling for him—crying out as though in pain.

He ran naked along the bank of the stream, out of the trees and around the bulk of the hut. In the dimness, two small figures flitted past him: fauns. But there—there between the red glow of the embers and the doorway of the hut—there were two larger figures on the ground, struggling.

As he reached them, one of the figures rose, backed away.

"Sorry—sorry," said Dymion. "I guess I got the wrong idea. A—a natural mistake."

Then he had backed farther away, and was gone, lost in the darkness.

But Meriam was there, lying face upward on the grass, exposed. As Mark knelt over her, he was shocked to see that she was nearly naked. She had lost her gown and sandals, and her sex was just covered by a fold of her undone waist-cloth. As she stirred now, reaching up for him, even this small covering fell away.

"Oh Mark—is it you?" she sobbed. "Mark, I didn't mean to. He thought—"

Mark took her by the shoulders, and she clung to him, her nipples brushing his chest.

"Oh Mark, forgive me! I only wanted to make you jealous—silly trick. And he nearly raped me. He pulled off my shoes, my gown—but you came in time, my dearest, my beloved."

"Beloved?" said Mark, caressing her hair, feeling the softness of her breasts against him. "Meri, do you really care for me—except as—well, you know . . ."

"I really care," she said, "I've really cared for a long long time. I *don't* care if you're not really any sort of Saint—maybe I'm not either. I—I just want to be your woman, Mark—your faithful woman. Your wife—if you like. If *you* want *me*. But maybe you prefer Helen."

"Blast Helen," said Mark, "she's a bitch. They're all bitches, these funny heathen. We're the same sort, Meri—we've been together long enough, in New Jay, for that. I—I don't know what came over me just now."

"I do," said Meriam. "He gave you some wild wine. Dextran native alcohol. When you and Helen were gone, he laughed, and told me it's a powerful aphrodisiac for humans. I didn't know that before. I'm glad I didn't have any. Because then maybe even I . . . but I didn't, Mark, I didn't, I'm still a virgin. I wanted to make sure I kept myself for you."

"There's one way you *can* make sure of that," said Mark with a sudden laugh. "That is, if you can forgive me for what I—just did. You can make sure, *now*."

"I forgive you everything, my darling," she said, and clasped him tightly, and kissed him on the lips. "Yes, yes . . ."

"Meri, my bride, my bride . . ."

"All right, Mark," she said, "make sure of me. Now."

The fire had subsided to a warm, comfortable glow, and the moons rode high in the south. And Mark and Meriam rose up, and went into the deeper darkness of the hut, and slept soundly there till dawn, in one another's arms.

Chapter Eight

There were chinks in the walls of the hut, and the golden fingers of dawn found them out. Meriam was still asleep beside him when Mark first stirred, and gently disengaged himself. He looked at her with a surge of tenderness: she was quite naked, naked as a little child, lying curled up there with her face and breasts hidden under one arm—an arm still circled with an aluminum bracelet.

Meri, my-sister-my-spouse—but really so, now. I must clothe her, he thought, protect her in this strange wild place.

He went out, naked himself, and retrieved her gown, undercloth and sandals, and brought them into the hut and laid them beside the sleeping girl. Then he went out again to hunt for his own lost clothing.

Out in the bay the *Naiad* was reassuringly there, and the sea was glass-still. There was a cluster of small fauns huddled in the beached rowboat, sitting quietly expectant of their masters' orders, their own revels now ended. A few meters off shore, an occasional rhythmic splash marked the progress of someone swimming as though for exercise. A man: yes, Dymion.

Mark turned his face to the jungle. Now it was a blaze of color—black tree trunks, purple foliage, masses of huge pink and white flowers. He headed into it along the stream, splashing through the shallow fresh water. On the forest edge, he stooped briefly to drink.

A great bass voice from the bushes above him:

"Is't you that ha' lost these strange green wees, young sir?"

Mark looked up, startled by the sound—and then fell back into the water, amazed utterly.

There stood before him a tall figure dressed only in a red cloak, and holding out his own crumpled jacket and trousers. But the figure was not a man—it was a centaur.

"Forgive me, fair sir," boomed the centaur, "mayhap I startled you—perchance you ha' not clapped eyes on one o' my quality before. I am Xathax, Speaker of the Wise Serpents, very much at your service. Are these by any chance your garments?"

"Yes," said Mark faintly, "yes." And he took them from Xathax's outstretched hand.

Now that he had got over his first shock at encountering a speaking centaur, he was checking Xathax's bodily features with a practiced eye. He stood a little higher than Mark himself—say, 175 centimeters, thus at least 10 centimeters taller than the tallest known species of centauroid. And he could *not* be very closely related—for all known centauroids were cat-footed or hooved on all feet, whereas Xathax's forefeet were extremely humanoid, apart from possessing only four toes to match his four-fingered hands. Plantigrade like a man in front, digitigrade like a cat behind—well, that was unusual, but made sense: Xathax needed a strong base in front to carry the weight of his heavy forebody.

Apart from that, he was not too surprising. He was gray-furred, with a dark-blue mass of head hair trailing into a short mane. Dark-blue equine tail to match. A head with a somewhat horsy muzzle, but rising at the back like a man's into a rounded brain case. Short pointed ears. A short blue beard. His only garment was a flowing crimson cloak, caught up around his shoulders by a cloth band.

Xathax watched him as he hurriedly got into his trousers and jacket. The centaur's expression was of course hard to interpret, but his mild brown eyes gave him an air of calm benevolence.

"Methinks I did not catch your name, young man," he said, as Mark finished.

"Oh—er—Mark Turner." He did not know what other ceremony was in order with centaurs, so he held out both hands. Xathax took both in his own four-fingered grip, held them briefly, and then released them.

"Why, that is wondrous courteous of you, young human," he said. "How did you come to know of our form in these matters?"

"I didn't," said Mark. "I guessed, Xa—Xa—"

"You may call me Handy," said the centaur, with something very like a smile on his mobile lips. "That is the meaning of Xathax, interpreted in your speech; it is also what Maister Dymion calls me."

Mark had just registered the fact that Dymion knew of Xathax's existence, when a couple of other figures came out of the bushes nearby. One was the green faun Hylo; the other was Helen. She was naked.

But not at all ashamed. She stared at Xathax, with wonder and admiration.

"Well, *well!*" she said. "Hylo warned me to expect a strange sight. He's magnificent. You'd better introduce me, Mark."

Mark did so, feeling overpowered by the impossibility of the situation. It was not every morning that one had to introduce one's naked ex-mistress to a centaur, while a faun stood by.

Once he had taken and dropped Helen's hands, Xathax turned to Mark.

"I was about to greet your captain when I encountered you, Sir Mark. Will ye take me to him now?"

"Follow me," said Mark. "Oh, Helen, you didn't see my boots anywhere, did you?"

She laughed. "They must be in the bushes somewhere, but I certainly haven't been looking. You'll have to find them yourself. Why did you have to rush off like that last night? No, don't tell me—I can guess. Well, no hard feelings: you two are much better suited, you know—*I* thought so all along. And I wasn't lonely without. I managed to console Dymion for his disappointment and then . . ." She shrugged—which, since she was naked, made an impressive gesture—and nodded slyly at Hylo. "Dymion told me you had a certain scientific query which he couldn't answer. The answer," she giggled, "is yes—if you work hard enough. Come on, Hylo, my love, you'd better help me find my own clothes."

When they reached the shore, Meriam was fully dressed and standing by the beached boat; she eyed Mark and the centaur with amazement. Dymion, not far off, was still half wet from the sea, dragging on his purple cloak. He looked surprised to see Xathax, but not nearly surprised enough.

"I happed to be on an embassy to the Southron tribe," explained Xathax mildly, "and then this morn caught sight of your argosy, Maister Dymion. You should be on your way to Flora; if't be so, will ye give me passage with you?"

"Come aboard, come aboard," growled Dymion. "I'm sorry if I sound surly, old Handy, but you catch us on the morning after—"

"A gaudy night?" said Xathax, nodding his muzzle with an air of understanding. "It is better to observe measure in such things, my friend. But proverbs are no salve for a sore head." He wandered off to greet the little fauns in the boat, and the humans were left alone for a moment.

"Mark," said Dymion, "I'm sorry about that silly little trick last night. I didn't realize that stuff would affect you so much. I've had it before—we keep a supply at Flora, and not only for the natives. As for what happened between me and Meriam—"

"That's all right," said Meriam softly. "Dymion and I have talked about that already, Mark—and we've apologized to each other. I was half to blame, you know. But," she added, breaking into a radiant smile, "I'm not really a bit sorry about the outcome!"

"What *was* the outcome?" asked Dymion. "You didn't tell me, Meriam."

"The outcome," said Mark, "is that Meri and I are engaged to be married—*really* engaged, I mean, by ourselves, not by a synod of family Saints."

"Congratulations, shipmates," said Dymion. "Mark, you dog-doctor, you don't deserve her—but I realize now I never had a chance; Meri's not the sharing type, and I rather guessed she was crazy about you when I first saw you both on the shore at Sunion. All right, then—I promise, no more passes at Puss-in-boots."

"I've given up boots," said Meriam, "and so has Mark, by the look of it."

Indeed, Mark never did find his boots at Nysa. For the rest of the voyage he had to go barefoot, which caused him no inconvenience.

Helen emerged clothed from the jungle, Hylo took his place in the rowboat without any overt scandal, they all returned to the ship, and the voyage was resumed—with the addition of Xathax. The weather was fine from now on, and the centaur would sleep on deck, wrapped only in his cloak.

"I suppose I owe you all an explanation about old Handy," said Dymion to Mark and Meriam once they were under way again. "The fact is, he was a trade secret, so to speak. I didn't want it known in Classica that there were rational centaurs in Anthis. That on top of new breeds of fauns—we'd be invaded, occupied by the Navy, our whole business would explode about us. I don't want that—I like things the way they are at Flora."

"You don't try to sell centaurs, then?" said Meriam drily. "Why not, if you're in the slaving business? They'd be the perfect farm animal—hexip and faun rolled into one, a self-propelled animate tractor and general mover, a handler too."

"Don't get me wrong," said Dymion. "I only sell slaves with their own advice and consent. The centaurs haven't offered themselves. They prefer to stay where they are."

"Tell me more," said Mark. "In fact, everything you know about them. Come on, Dymion, this is *my* sort of business!"

"Well—they turned up soon after we came to Anthis, four years ago. In fact, they helped us build Flora—it was quite hard work, and as you say, they are perfect general movers. I taught them their English, of course—you recognize the style? But they already had a sort of language of their own at that time—unlike the fauns. They claimed they had only recently evolved it, with some inspiration from us—whatever that means. I think it can only mean that they're witches like us Lees—they've picked up the idea of language from human minds on this planet. Believe it or not—but I do believe it; in fact, I have the impression that a lot of native creatures are good at that sort of witchcraft, they *communicate* with each other better than we do."

"That's heresy," said Mark nervously, "and I don't mean just that the Saints say so—I'd rather not accept it till I see it proved. But as regards Dextran creatures, I'm aware of that idea already. It cropped up right after the Landing. But go on."

"Well, there's not much more. Our centaurs' main home is north of Flora, where the Anthis forest begins to thin out into the grasslands of that so well-named plain, Centauria. They are not plains grazers—they like to browse on trees, fruit, nuts, and so on. I think they can eat meat, but they prefer not to. They've got a little culture of their own—small villages in forest clearings. They've learned to weave cloth since we arrived; in fact they supply us now in the stead. Altogether, they're incredibly useful to us, since they're so friendly, so dextrous, and so strong. I don't believe we could run Flora even now without them."

"And what do *they* get out of all this?" said Meriam. "They're not your slaves, are they?"

"No. And neither are the fauns, really. Both lots just come out of the forest, and volunteer to help. They seem to like our company—we amuse them, or something. You'll see how it is when we arrive."

"All right," said Meriam, "just one more thing. If the centaurs are a trade secret—*why are we here?* You know Mark's a zoologist! Once he publishes—"

Dymion shrugged. "Yes, I know—we get busted. Frankly, I'm puzzled about that, too. But here I'm trusting the old family witchcraft—it's my father's hunch, he wanted someone like you to come 'for the greater good of everybody,' as he put it—and I'm willing to go along with that. My father's still head of the stead in theory, and so far whatever he's suggested has turned out right—so I'll follow his lead this time, too."

Mark had been wondering what the sleeping arrangements might be now in the *Naiad*'s cabins. As soon as he could, he drew Meriam aside on the poop deck and made a certain suggestion. But Meriam stood out for the *status quo*.

"No, dear," she whispered, "we're still not *married*, and before strangers . . . Besides, I don't want to encourage Helen to—to go with Dymion."

Mark smiled, and nodded toward the lower, forward deck, where they could see Helen engrossed in conversation with Xathax. "I don't think she's likely to extend her favors to Dymion again. She seems to have lost interest in mere *humans*."

"I don't believe that," said Meriam. "Poor girl, she's a strange type. I think she's looking for a man *like her*, and so far she's found no one. We had some serious talks together in that cabin these last few nights, you know. I felt I could have killed her, sometimes—when she admitted she'd enjoyed you, and might do so again—but I was relieved, too: she wasn't seriously after you. I don't think she's really a bad girl—well, not *wicked*—though some of the things she said! That business with Hylo—well, that wasn't her first attempt."

"What!"

"No. That one night after her punishment—after the new fauns had been landed in Sunion—she said she tried to seduce a *couple* of the males—Tages and Telkin, or some such names. She didn't succeed. She told me, 'Fauns are bad lovers—not at all like the old myths'! I think she, well, went with Hylo that time to try to prove something What, I don't know."

"Possibly scientific curiosity. Well, science should be grateful to her—if she's telling the truth about her success. I expect she is—as she said, as long as you try hard enough. But as for their being bad lovers, that's what I would have expected. Since we have different proteins and so on, I don't suppose we even *smell* right to them." Mark smiled grimly. "But maybe Dextra's working on *that* problem, too."

"Mark, whatever do you mean?"

"I—well, I just think it's uncanny, the way these fauns keep on getting more human-seeming with every new species. What sort of superfauns are we going to find in Flora?"

Meriam shuddered, with a touch of exaggeration. "Mark, darling, you'll have to protect me from them!"

He laughed and hugged her. "Let 'em come near you, and I'll get out my laser. I don't believe in sharing my girl."

Meriam gradually confided in Mark about other matters. How she had been in love with him for years, but had felt constrained and shy in the false relationship set up by that arranged marriage. And how she had long doubted the sacredness of the Lordist religion.

"I could only admit *that* to myself," she said, "after I had got friendly with those Sunion women. Talk about sociology! I can't write them up truly; I'll have to lie and lie, fake it up with jargon."

"Don't worry, that's quite common in sociology," said Mark. "You'll do well."

"Yes. Well, those 'heathen' converted *me!* Especially Cynthia. I'm a heathen, now, Mark."

"Oh yeah?" said Mark. "Then sleep with me at once, you abandoned hussy!"

She smiled. "You're right, darling—I'm not a heathen all the way. Only half."

"Never mind, my little Saint, I love you the way you are. *Because* you are the way you are. There's *some* good in the Lordist way of life, only it's distorted, exaggerated. When we are married, my sweet, I'd like us both to settle in Atlantis as soon as we can afford to."

"You quoted the right text at me before, Mark," said Meriam softly. "Whither thou goest . . ."

The morning after their Midsummer madness, Monday, July 1, they had a steady north wind on their port quarter, the coast of Anthis trending southeast by east. The breeze kept the heat bearable. A couple of kilometers to starboard, the land was already thick purple jungle. Flora lay at the very end of the southeastern gulf of the Euxin; Dymion reckoned they should reach it in a couple of days.

Their skipper had returned to his role of seagoing sobriety. As Mark and Meriam sat together on the poop deck, he now appeared and took over the helm from Hylo. He waved cheerfully to the young couple, and pointed over the ship's side.

"Fine dolphin weather," he said.

Yes, there were the dolphins—that is, native pseudodelphs. A whole school of them were streaking past, overtaking the ship, showing their backs at times above the milky blue water.

"I'm glad the Fisheries men haven't poisoned them—yet," said Mark. He got to his feet. "I think I'd like now to interview another life form—old Handy. Anyone seen him?"

"Try the cabins," called Dymion. "I last saw him going in there with Helen."

Mark was wondering whether he ought to go any

farther, when at that moment Xathax emerged on the lower deck, heading toward the bow. The centaur was normally quite surefooted aboard the ship, but now his movements seemed uneasy. Mark went down and met him.

"Ah, fair sir," said Xathax. "Is't true, as I am told, that you are learned in the ways of life?"

"I study animals. That's why I wanted to put a few questions to you, Handy, about yourself and your people."

"And the human animal, do you study that too? Dost know thy own self? My friend, I could e'en profit by some counsel. If't please you, I would tell you a tale and pose you some questions, and then, if you will, do you question me."

"Fair enough," said Mark.

There were some fauns about, but they walked on around the small forward deck till the billowing mainsail hid them from everyone farther aft, and the flapping of the foresail and the whine of the wind gave their conversation complete privacy. Then Xathax began.

"Sir Mark, I have till this day known only one of your human females, and that was the Lady Rosina of Flora. The Lady Rosina is gracious, and composed, and indeed might compare with some of our own centaur ladies; but this young Mistress Helen—why, I fear her mind's diseased, her fancy blasted with the very ecstasy of madness—or are there many more like her?"

"Not many, I don't think so—but go on. What has she been up to?" said Mark, already guessing.

"Sir, all today she has made much of me, praising—forsooth—my handsomeness, which indeed cannot be much since I am somewhat declined into the vale of years."

"Oh yes?" said Mark, interested. "How old are you?"

"Near eighty winters."

"Why, you seem in the prime of life," said Mark, astounded. No known centauroids lived beyond fifty.

"We do not live much beyond an hundred years," said Xathax, as though guessing his thought, "but our old age is tolerably hale, if we keep within a moderate diet and receive the blessings of the forest. But now to my tale. Praising, as I say, my handsome form, the Lady Helen led me into her chamber, where there was then no other creature, and began to talk of love. She opined that I must keep satisfied a great number of lusty females of my own kind, and similar nonsense, whereas indeed I have but one wife, as is our nature, and do not desire any other."

"Don't tell me you mate monogamously for life," said Mark. "Like some birds."

"But we do, fair sir, precisely that. And I told the maiden so. The Lady Helen said she found this hard of belief, and wondered if I might not like to *try a change*. Then she quoted me one of your old tales, a most absurd story of centaurs lusting after human women, and indeed carrying off human brides by violence and in drink. Sir, this is a vile calumny: we are no winebibbers, and take not above a single cup of an evening when we wish to keep our human hosts at Flora in countenance. As for lusting after two-legged females—why, the thing is absurd. I observed to Mistress Helen that there would in any case be grave difficulties of a mechanical nature, seeing that the human mode is, I am told, face to face, whereas with us the parts of love are far behind, convenient for mounting. A centaur who wished to accost a two-legged lady should have his virile member before, between his front legs—a monster, sir, which does not exist in Nature. Also, I might add, as you can see, we real centaurs are somewhat largely endowed, which might occasion some pain for the two-legged inamorata."

Mark laughed. "Yes indeed. Well, what did she say to that?"

Xathax stroked his dark blue beard, and looked, if possible, embarrassed. "Sir, she said very little, except, 'Why don't you try,' or some such speech, and assured me she was willing to risk a little pain for my love—and then, Sir, she took off her garments and embraced me. Fair sir, I do not wish to seem discourteous—your human shape, which is much like the shape of a faun, has no doubt a certain beauty, especially when the faun or human is clambering about in the trees for which it is so clearly designed. But for a female lacking in one pair of limbs—and equipped with those strange external milk glands—for such to aspire to be a centaur's love! Worse still, in truth, the lack of a mingling mind—"

"Eh?" said Mark. "I don't follow that."

Xathax looked at him gravely. "No—I might suppose not. But let be: perchance you will hereafter. Well, to cut my tale short, I requested the Lady Helen to unhand me, since I would not be unfaithful to Xilifil, my dear wife, even if I could, which with *her* I certainly could not, whereupon, she flung away into the other cabin, and I thought it best to come out here, wondering, indeed, if the poor girl was not stark crazed in the brain, and if there were not any medicine that might recover her. I myself have some skill in leechcraft, and have ministered to distempers in the young of my tribe; but I have seen no malady any whit like this. What think you, Sir Mark? Is this disorder common among human females, and is there any easy cure?"

"No," said Mark, "it's not common. I've not known anyone quite like Helen. I believe she is discontented with being a human—what the cure for that is, I don't know."

"Ah," said Xathax, brooding, "this is clearly a matter beyond the powers of us little movers. But we need not despair. There is healing and renewing in our forests."

Xathax restored his composure partly by taking instruction from Dymion, and becoming a member of the working crew of the ship. He was soon a good sailor, equally handy with rope or helm, and of course stronger at his tasks than anyone else. He was especially good at the wheel, steering a course nearly as straight as a laser beam, his large hands gripping firmly, his four feet well planted on the deck. He also very much enjoyed being helmsman.

At the humans' supper that evening, in the rear cabin, Dymion said, "If ever the centaurs come out of hiding in their forests, they should have a fine career in sail ships. They've got just the right temperament. Strong, sober—not like me! Under sail I have to assume a virtue, but truly I have it not. Not many of us do, to that extent. The centaurs of the old Earth myths mostly got a very bad press."

"Depends how you look at it," said Helen wryly. "I wouldn't mind having at least *one* of those *mythical* centaurs around."

"Nor would I," agreed Dymion. "At least, around Flora—they certainly sounded colorful! But there was also a minority opinion on centaurs, you know, *not* stressing their unruliness. Xathax rather fits that—he's so integrated. Here, let me read you a piece of verse."

He reached up into the cabin's bookshelf, and opened a large battered-looking book and read:

"Harmonious Monster, whose strange Shape
Commits on Kind most pleasant rape,
Both Man and Beast may envy thee
Thy four-footed dexterity.
This Steed his eyes to Heav'n may raise
And take his meat with hands, not graze:
This Man forgets not to be wise
In the Earth's deep humilities,
And planted firm, fears not at all
To stumble, or like *Adam* fall;
So well may he be call'd alone
Of Animals the Paragon;

Apotheosis of the Horse,
Matchless to run, stand or discourse.
Alas, for Fancy! this bright *Plan*
Of better Horse, of stabler Man,
Our Stepdame World of duller Earth
Could not conceive, or bring to birth . . .

"See what I mean?"

Helen made a face. "Not *my* kind of centaur, that."

"I like your poem, Dymion," said Meriam. "Is there more of it?"

"There's more, but I don't want to bore Helen, you can read it for yourself. Anyway, it's not *my* poem, it's an old Earthly, anonymous seventeenth-century, I found it on a loose leaf in a second-hand book—"

"Don't you believe it, Meri," laughed Helen. "That's one of Dymion's typical little jokes. He will make up these fakes himself and try to pass them off as old Earthly."

"It's in print," protested Dymion, waving the leaf.

"So what? I know you've got a hand press at Flora!"

"Oh well," said Dymion, "does it matter? If someone didn't write that poem in the seventeenth century, they should have. The centaur symbol—"

Helen yawned. "Now you *are* being a bore, Dimmy: you're nicer when you're drunk. Why should *you* write moldy old poems about being stable, etcetera?"

"I admire stability," said Dymion solemnly, "especially in other people. As for myself, I pray like old St. Augustine—'Lord, make me chaste, *but not yet*.' If you like me drunk, Helly, just wait till we get to Flora."

It was late, but for Mark and Meriam sleeping now meant parting. They went up on deck. The night was fine, and Xathax at the helm waved to them as they leaned on the rail under the ship's stern lantern.

"Give you good even, Sir Mark, Lady Meriam," he boomed.

They returned his greeting. "He's nice," said Meriam, turning back to Mark. "I wonder what his wife's like?"

"Gray-furred and eighty years old and no breasts," said Mark, laughing softly. "Each to his taste—I prefer my own she." He gripped her hand. "Darling, our worthy helmsman won't be embarrassed by a couple of bipeds kissing *each other*. . . ."

"Mark, it's Monday—the Sabbath," said Meriam, with mock severity, when they had kissed. "You don't want me to drop all my Livyan traditions, do you? No, you don't, you've said so before. Well, I've never let a Sabbath go by before without reading some Scripture. Don't you think we might . . ."

She held up the green-covered, familiar book in the light of the lantern.

"OK," said Mark, "let's read it together. So long as you choose the Song of Songs which is of Solomon. That was always my favorite portion."

They held the book together, hands clasped on the opened pages.

"Let him kiss me with the kisses of his mouth—" began Meriam.

"For thy love is better than wine," added Mark, looking not at the book but at his girl. "I know most of this by heart, darling."

PART THREE: *The Fauna of Flora*

Chapter Nine

On the afternoon of July 3, a hot bright day, they came to their destination.

The coastline had swung north across their course, and now stood like a widely curving wall barring their way eastward. The ship was almost embraced in a huge bay. At this inmost reach of the Euxin gulf of Tethys, the land of New Asia came purple-forested right down to the sea, the black trunks of paramangroves actually rising out of salt water. The only gap in the jungle was an ample river mouth.

The eight little blue fauns were huddled in a group amidships, silently gazing at their native forest. The centaur, Xathax, and the green fauns, Hylo and Huon, stood by, forward, to handle the sails. Meanwhile, the humans were all on the poop, with Dymion as pilot managing the wheel. He was heading the *Naiad* straight towards the river mouth.

"The Serpent River," he announced. "Flora lies up there, on the south bank, just around the first bend. Here we go!"

Meriam took Mark's hand. They were both dressed in

their Agency uniforms, Mark of course barefoot, Meriam back in her boots, since her Sunion sandals were too big for secure walking, and right now she felt the need of a little security.

"Oh Mark," she whispered, "doesn't it look jungly! Wild! The *Serpent* River . . ."

"Don't worry, Meri," laughed Mark. "Native Dextran serpents don't bite humans, and they're nonpoisonous anyway." He looked at her with obvious affection in his handsome brown eyes.

Oh, how nice he was, her lover! And strong, and expert, and reassuring. With him by her side, she wouldn't be afraid to go to the uttermost west or the uttermost east, to Atlantis—or Anthis. Not even though Anthis was the exact opposite of her dear safe green native land. Not even though it held the Serpent River.

In the New Scriptures, for which she still had an ingrained reverence, there had been two Tempters in the Garden: for Eve, the Serpent; for Adam, Lilith. This land looked as though it might well belong to both of them.

What form of Lilith might lie in wait here for Mark? She looked askance at Helen, golden-tanned, bare-limbed Helen laughing in the vague radiance of Dextran day, her eyes eager with obvious desire for the shore and what it might bring. Well, it jolly well wouldn't bring her *Mark* again. Mark might be susceptible to female charms, but not to anything as crude as Helen had revealed herself to be. One good point about Anthis: there were no tempting females here.

Well, at least no *human* ones . . .

Almost the first thing Mark noticed about Flora was the swarm of creatures awaiting them on the wooden river dock: mostly the bigger green fauns and those females of theirs, the pretty blue-haired nymphs. Nice to see some of *those* again! There were also a sprinkling of centaurs, who stood out easily because of their height; several smaller creatures, which might be household pets; and one human woman in a long white Classican gown, who must be Rosina Lee, Dymion's wife. She stood there surrounded by the rational and irrational animals like Eve in Paradise ringed with friendly beasts.

It was not easy to pick out the stead itself. He had trouble seeing it, because the long low house was built not of stone but of dark native logs, with a roof of faded purple-and-blue thatch.

"Not bad, is it?" said Dymion proudly, tying a mooring rope. "We put it up ourselves, four years ago, with native materials and native help. Blends in well, doesn't it?"

It did indeed. There were some Earthly-green cultivated plants and fruit trees in plantations behind and to the right of the house, but they seemed to have been systematically sown or set between rows of purple and blue vegetation.

"It's handy that way," explained Dymion. "In fact, both sorts do better so, I think. Their respective pests have to fly farther to get from one edible plant to the next. That makes for fertile farming."

"I believe some people do the same in Atlantis," said Mark. "But—but this is not *very* like Atlantis. As you said, much more lush. More *purple*."

He could disentangle the various welcoming creatures better now. No, there were no little blue fauns, only greenskins like Hylo and Huon. Many of these—all the females—were covered from the waist down in red or purple cloths knotted like sarongs; others were naked; and most of the clothed as well as the naked ones wore diadems of purple leaves and bright gold flowers tucked into their thick blue head hair. A riot of gaudy color! The centaurs, too, were of several colors in their fur—brown, gray, blue. He guessed that some were females—the ones with flowers in their manes—and a closer look confirmed this. That gray-furred centaur lady waving to Xathax must surely be Xilifil, though she did not look eighty years old.

The smaller beasts included excited, barking paracans; a squawking red-and-yellow handibird perched on the shoulder of a faun; a dog-sized, fierce-looking reptile with leathery wings; and another winged beast like a flying cat.

Rosina was a woman of about her husband's age, twenty-eight or thirty, good-looking in a quiet way. Brown hair, calm gray eyes. Now as they landed Dymion had gone up to her, kissed her, whispered. Then Rosina stepped forward to meet her guests, who were being gaped at by the crowd of native creatures.

"Don't mind our local friends," she said with a smile. "They're only inquisitive. Ah, Helen—well, I know you, child, but how you've grown! I thought you would turn up here someday. And you two—you are the Turners?"

Mark made the introductions.

"Zoologist?" said Rosina, glancing from Mark to the fauns and centaurs. "You've got a rich field for study here, Mark, and I mustn't grudge it you—Lucius said someone like you would be coming. The fauns, of course, will be known abroad already anyway; but—are you going to tell the whole truth in your reports?"

Mark exchanged glances with Meriam. "I—I certainly wouldn't want to damage your way of life here. It's beautiful."

"Knowledge is often damaging to what is beautiful," said Rosina. "I try not to know too much about some things—it's best to let them follow their own development undisturbed." She looked briefly at her husband, with the ghost of a sad smile on her lips. "But enough of that—I'm glad to see you, all of you. Ah, old Handy, how nice . . ."

"You will excuse us, will you not, Lady Rosina?"

boomed Xathax. He was arm in arm with Xilifil, and clustered about by the other centaurs. "I am expected by my people, to give an account of my embassage. We shall encounter again, anon, at tomorrow's feast." And with that, and many bows, the centaurs disentangled themselves from the crowd and began trotting up the riverbank.

"Excuse me too, a minute," said Dymion. "I have to see to my fauns." Hylo and Huon were already lost among the other greenskins, but Dymion had turned back to talk to the eight little blues, who looked dwarfed and lonely among their bigger relations.

"What are these other creatures?" asked Meriam, looking around. "That—that scaly thing . . ."

"That's our pet dragon," said Rosina. "Fafner. His wings aren't very powerful, but he can just about get off the ground, like a big chicken. He's quite harmless—eats mainly beetles. And the flying cat—we call them sphinxes—she's Felissa."

Felissa arched her back, jumped, flapped her furry wings, and was airborne, landing after a short flight on the thatched roof of the building. There she turned and regarded them with bright yellow eyes, her purple pelt bristling.

Rosina laughed. "We've got several sphinxes—they're good paramousers. I expect Felissa will get friendlier to you later. You'll see up at the house, Dymion has carved portraits of her and Fafner. Come, let's go there now, and settle you in. The fauns will take your bags." She looked down at their feet and smiled. "Why is one of you barefoot, and the other in boots?"

"It's a long story," said Meriam hastily. "Mark lost his footgear, and the only sandals I've got are too big."

"We can fix you both up, I think," said Rosina. "Mark's feet look about the same size as Dymion's, and yours, Meriam, about the same as mine."

They tramped the short distance from the landing stage to the house. The front of the building consisted of a main block in the center with long wings of open wooden galleries or railed verandas leading to other blocks right and left. At intervals before the verandahs, and on either side of the central doorway, there stood statues carved in light-gray stone—alternately native dragons and sphinxes.

And then the main door opened from within, and a man stood in the entrance.

"Ah, at last," said Rosina. "Here's Lucius."

Lucius Lee had the usual black eyes and high cheekbones of his family, but his face was lined, drawn, his hair and wispy beard white. He wore a long blue-and-purple robe. Mark thought he looked very like a wizard as portrayed in the old Earthly books.

He fixed Mark and Meriam with his dark yet glittering gaze. "I knew there would be strangers. Two in green, eh? Just as I dreamed. Well, you are not unexpected. Flora will know how to welcome you." And with that he turned on his heel and disappeared into the building.

"Don't let my father-in-law disturb you," said Rosina, with a little smile. "He's an old eccentric, and a bit of a recluse. His den's at the back of the house, and he doesn't often emerge from it, except for strolls in the forest, or for meals—and not even always for those."

"Where's Kim?" said Helen. "When I last saw him, we were both just kids. I've been looking forward to meeting him again."

"Sorry," said Dymion, coming forward. "Rosy was telling me earlier—my wandering kid brother's wandering again. Literally, I mean—he's been off in the forest somewhere for a couple of days. Don't worry, that's normal for him now. He'll show up in due course. Now, come on in—I don't know about you, but I'm famished. When's dinner, Rosy?"

The stead-house was a strange place, not only in being built of dark native wood, but also in plan. It was hardly a single building at all, but a number of wooden, thatched pavilions connected by gallery-corridors or in some cases by mere roofed tubolia-wood colonnades laid out through the gardens behind the main front. Still other pavilions were quite isolated, and reached by stepping-stone paths across blue lawns. "Indoors" and "outdoors" were concepts that hardly applied. Even the largest single block, the dining hall in the center of the façade, had wide-open windows on which small handibirds perched and chattered. In the gardens were banks of enormous gaudy native flowers, stone-bordered fishponds, and more stone statues—of fauns and other Dextran creatures.

"It's soft local stone," said Rosina, conducting them. "Dymion carved some to start with, and then the centaurs learned, and did some more."

"It's all incredibly beautiful," said Mark, looking around at the gardens. "There's nothing, nothing like this in Livya. The Saints don't hold with 'graven images.' "

"Why aren't there any graven images of *humans?*" asked Meriam.

"Well," said Rosina, "Lucius is our general artistic director, you know, and he says this is not really a country for humans at all, we're just guests here. I often think he's right. I'm from West Classica myself—Dymion and I met in Eirenis—and my own background is much more civilized than all this. I put up with it, for Dymion's sake. I put up with a lot of things for Dymion's sake. For instance," she added hastily, "I miss my children, but we can't get radio school here. Not that I don't like Flora—the native creatures are very charming—but . . ." She shrugged. "Oh well, you'll see."

Meriam held Mark's hand as Rosina led them over a stepping-stone path to a pavilion isolated in the grounds. A couple of male fauns followed, carrying their luggage.

"I hope you'll like your room—" began Rosina.

"Please, are you short of rooms?" said Meriam quickly.

"No—there are several spare. Why?"

"We—we'd like separate rooms," said Meriam. "We're promised—not married yet."

Rosina smiled. "Are your Saintly Elders breathing down your necks, then, even at this distance? But have it your own way. I must say, for that matter I do like a little modesty in girls—and in boys. All right, Meriam, I'll give Mark the room which is the other half of this pavilion. There's a partition wall, and a door through it which you can keep locked or not as you please. And now, let's show you the facilities."

The "facilities" were extremely primitive. On the wooden floor in each room was a mattress, and in one corner a washstand, basin and ewer. Not far off in the garden was a little hut-lavatory, of a type Mark and Meriam had only seen before in work camps in the Livyan hills.

"If you want a bath," said Rosina, "you'll have to use the river. It's safe, and clean: the maids will show you the best places to use. Ah, here they are."

The male fauns had dumped the luggage and disappeared, but now the "maids" came around the corner of the pavilion, bowing and smiling. They were two green-skinned faun-girls ("Nymphs," thought Mark), dark-blue-haired, with neat pointed ears and violet eyes, dressed in crimson sarongs but nothing above the waist. The tops of their heads came up to Mark's chin.

"Meet Chloe and Circe," said Rosina. "They're the chambermaids for this pavilion."

"Well met, good-den, Maister, Mistress," chorused Chloe and Circe.

Rosina sighed. "We all have to put up with this style of English, I'm afraid. Dymion thought it a good joke at the time, using Elizabethan play texts as teaching materials, and now the natives have got stuck with it. I hope you don't mind."

Mark beamed. "I don't mind a bit—I've had some experience of it already. Hel-lo, you two, nice to see you."

It was some time since he'd had a chance to examine greenskin nymphs properly. Yes, the resemblance to human girls was striking. The purple lips and nipples were shapely, the four-toed feet ditto, the breasts . . .

Meriam nudged him sharply. "How do we tell one from the other?"

"I'm Chloe," said Chloe.

"I'm Circe," said Circe.

They were indeed remarkably alike. "Twins?" guessed Mark.

"Yes," said Rosina, "I believe it's common with them."

"It's *normal,*" said Mark, "at least in the earlier species, and now I guess in this one—single births are the rarity."

"I am your maid, Mistress," said Circe. "Chloe is Master Mark's girl."

"No, she's not," snapped Meriam, "*I* am! Get that straight, both of you little—"

Rosina laughed. "She doesn't mean what you think, Meriam. They won't make passes at human boys—they're not designed that way." She paused, as though choosing her words carefully. "On the other hand, they're very obliging."

"Did you say 'designed'?" asked Mark. "What do you mean?"

"Oh . . . nothing. I'll leave you to wash now, and then—dinner in ten minutes."

While they were washing, the maids disappeared and returned almost at once with two pairs of sandals and armfuls of colored cloths. The sandals fitted nicely.

"What are all those for?" asked Meriam, nodding at the cloths.

"For Maister and Mistress," chorused the maids. "Fine robes for ye both to dine in."

"All worthily woven and daintily dyed," added Circe, "by four-legged ladies, most skillful centauresses."

Mark picked up a purple toga. "Why, I rather fancy this—bit of a change from my uniform!"

Meriam laughed. "You will look gorgeous, my love. Ah, I'm glad there's a green robe—that's for me. This place brings out my Livyan nationalism. Oh! What's that?"

A sphinx the size of a large Earthly cat had landed with a whirr of wings on the windowsill, and crouched there blinking its yellow eyes at them.

"Don't worry," said Mark. "I've handled them before. Puss, puss . . ."

He tickled the sphinx under its chin. It shut its eyes, and purred.

Shadows were deepening when the Lees and their guests assembled in the dining hall, and Rosina ordered the faun serving boys to light the oil lamps that hung on aluminum chairs from the wooden ceiling. The room might have been gloomy in the flickering lamplight, had it not been for the walls, which were painted bright yellow. Their surface was dotted with a dark-brown design, a repeated motif of a cross or plus sign with a small disk at its center.

The layout of the room was like the dining hall at Sunion, but without separation of sexes. There were three double couches, and one thronelike chair with arms carved into a semblance of flower petals. Rosina and Dymion shared one couch, Mark and Meriam were given another, while Helen was left solitary on the third; Lucius arrived later than anybody else, and took the throne.

"My father's a bit of an ascetic," murmured Dymion to Mark, "and he also likes to be impressive. Hence the throne. Glory before comfort, for him."

The style of the little feast, Mark thought, was going to

be much as in Classica; but the dim lamps and dark wooden ceiling and floor reminded him that they were in another and wilder country. Lucius' throne too was a strange touch; and that wall motif was beginning to bother him.

"Why the plus signs?" he remarked, as soon as they were all settled in their places.

Lucius regarded him fixedly. "Young man, I am glad you said that. A good omen: the right question implies the right quester. Observe: the disk has *four arms*. What does that suggest?"

"To me it suggests a cross," put in Meriam. "That's part of our Livyan flag, along with the Crescent and Menorah. But surely you wouldn't be so Saintly . . ."

"The Cross," said Lucius coldly, "is a symbol not reserved to your limited religion. But I am still waiting to hear from *Master* Turner."

Mark said, "Here's a silly idea. But if you will ask a scientist . . . it reminds me of a diagram of the carbon atom. Four little rods for the valences."

Lucius' eyes gleamed. "The nucleus, the essential structure of Life itself. Good, good! You seem very promising, young man. That may not be the full answer; but let that go for now. We may have good hopes of you."

This exchange did not exactly put Mark at his ease. Flora and its inhabitants were turning out stranger, wilder even than he had expected. He was almost relieved to find that the food and wine, now being brought in, were human-type, not Dextran. He remarked as much to the company in general.

"Yes," said Rosina, "we've not gone native to that extent yet! Tomorrow we'll hold a proper feast—it's an ancient High Day of Earth history, according to Lucius—and we'll invite some centaurs. Then we'll have to watch the servants—sometimes they make a mistake and mix up the Dextran and Earthly fruits and vegetables. Sing out, please, everybody, if that happens to you."

"Sure," said Helen, with a shudder; and Mark knew that she was remembering the taste of golden apple.

"What *is* tomorrow's feast actually in honor of?" asked Meriam.

"Independence," said Lucius gravely from his throne. "Once on Earth, the ancestors of the First Hundred had colonized a new continent. For well over a century they were mere colonists, subordinate, tied to their mother country over a vast space of waters. Then they realized that they could manage on their own. They were no longer second-hand Europeans, but *Americans*—natives of their New World. So, one Fourth of July, they declared themselves Independent of their former world, different, free."

"Which we'll never be," said Helen sadly. "Not in *our* New World. Oh, I know we're vastly separated from Earth—Old Earth is gone for ever. But physically, we're bound to that damned planet. We'll never be true Dextrans. Our chemistry, our whole *build* is against us. I envy those." And she pointed to the green fauns and nymphs who were moving lithely among the tables, clearing the dishes for the next course.

"Do you really?" said Meriam. "*I* don't, Helen. First of all, we're not doing too badly as we are. It's true we're confined to the bits of the planet which have been Apple-seeded or at least planted with some green crops, but that needn't be a great hardship if we don't increase our population much more. I agree now with Mark," she said shyly, "that we shouldn't. The four-children law ought to be dropped soon. As to *build*—well, we're adapting, you know. You're unlucky, Helen, to be so tall and fair; most of us now are turning out shorter and darker, and with nice thick ankles. I expect in time the *Dextran* human race will be no taller than those fauns, but maybe chunkier. Isn't that likely, Mark?"

"More than likely—it's a certainty," said Mark. "The differential mortality mostly hit the tall fair boy babies. Even though the First Hundred were nearly all fairish Caucasians, we're going to end up looking like the Malays of Old Earth—short, stocky and brown."

"Rough luck for me in the meantime," said Helen. "Anyway, we'll never be truly *native*. Not like the fauns."

"*Are* they true natives?" said Mark. "I'm not sure of that."

Everyone looked at him in astonishment, except possibly Lucius, whose expression was unfathomable. Meriam said, "Well, if they're not natives, they're pretty good imitations!"

"Good imitations," said Mark, musing. "Lord of Landers, yes! That's just how they strike me. Imitations! But of what?"

"Young man," said Lucius, "explain yourself."

"I'm not sure that I can. I'm groping—you know more about these folk than I do. Look—shall we leave it till dinner's over?"

He nodded at the faun servants; and the others took his meaning. When the servants had left the after-dinner wine and retired, Mark said:

"One of the things which has most struck me about fauns—including the earlier sort, the blueskins—is their lack of individuality. Most animals vary a good deal—physically, temperamentally. The fauns don't. There's so little range, it's hard to tell them apart, one boy from another boy, one girl from another girl. And I don't mean just between the pairs of twins, like Chloe and Circe, though maybe their twinning is somehow part of the same general thing—Chloe and Circe are hardly an eyelash different from a faun-girl called Florimel, whom I studied in Sunion. And the waiters we had here tonight—I would have been in real trouble trying to distinguish them. Yet I wouldn't be boasting if I told you I'm *good* at distinguishing individual animals—it's my line, after all. I can tell one paracan pup from another in any litter, one sphinx kitten from another pretty easily. But these fauns! They're weird."

He paused. Hell! There was another thing. Even spookier. He continued:

"Look, perhaps you others—Dymion, Rosina—you can help me on this. The fauns—blues and greens—they speak English quite fluently now, to us. *But I can't remember ever hearing one faun speaking to another when a human wasn't involved in the conversation!* Have any of you seen them do so?"

Rosina shook her head. "No. When they sit together, they sit in silence; when they kiss and caress, they do so in silence; when they work together, even at complicated tasks, they manage fine, without ever speaking a word. The most they ever do, when they're relaxing, is to burble or babble a little. I'm surprised, really, that they can speak to *us*. Themselves, they don't seem to need words."

"Not for intercommunication," agreed Lucius calmly, "only for thinking. We have helped the faun-world think, and it's grateful for that."

Mark stared at Lucius, but said nothing. The old man continued:

"Nor do all humans always need words. But in humans, the deeper communion is rare. They *mis*understand each other—whence springs much sorrow. Perhaps such sorrow must always be for all left-handed, Earth-type life. But my experience of Dextra—and I've wandered the blue plains and purple forests a good deal in all my time—my experience, I say, is that on this planet, where life has taken a different direction from the beginning—here there is a wide and deep mingling of mind."

Dymion laughed. "My father says it more impressively,

Mark, but I said that before—they're all witches, like us Lees, only more so. The centaurs—and the fauns."

"All right," said Mark, "let's assume that the fauns have ESP. I'm not sure that's the right way of putting it, though. Do ants have ESP? It's rather that they're parts of a nest, a society in which the individuals don't count for anything *but* parts. Now I'm not saying that fauns are as low in individuality as ants, but they're getting on that way. And that's not the end of it. My main point is this. They don't strike me as *natural* animals. Apart from the weird way new types keep on emerging from this jungle, *what other Dextran animal is green*? All right, I'll tell you: one or two handibirds—species of pseudoparrot. The exceptions prove the rule, because those birds are green for *conspicuous coloring*. But there are no green mammals. The earlier types of faun—and the still-earlier gobblers—they were reasonably colored, camouflaged for Dextran vegetation, blue-skinned and purple-haired. And now suddenly—these little green men! It's my belief there were *no* greenies before the human Landing. I think they're adaptations—or imitations."

"Imitations of what?" said Helen.

"Of us—or of something in our minds. The first gobblers were nothing like humans to look at, and to our eyes they were ugly. Each new kind has been getting prettier, more human-looking. This last lot are now very like the old mythical stereotype—they're mimicking Earth-classical fauns and dryads. It's uncanny."

"Couldn't they be just adapting to the new green vegetation?" said Meriam.

"What, so that they can gambol in Earthly forests? That's a nice idea," said Mark. "No—actually it's not, it's a *frightening* idea. Because they've been adapting *here*, in Anthis, where there's *no* green forest—would you say, Meri, so they can slip unobtrusively into the forests of Classica—or Livya?"

"Wouldn't that be fun," laughed Helen, "green nymphs running about those work camps and stirring up those old Saints of yours!"

"One more thing," said Mark. "Dymion, what's happened to the bulk of our old crew? Those eight blueskins who came back with us on the *Naiad?*"

"Gone," said Dymion. "They thanked me politely, and then scampered off into the forest. Springol said, 'We are going to our long home.' "

Mark felt Meriam tense against him. The little blue demon had quoted from Scripture, and a grisly text at that! Yet certainly no one in Sunion or at sea had taught him Ecclesiastes. . . . He grasped Meriam by the hand to comfort her. And then there came an interruption.

A figure had entered the shadowy room. At first glance Mark thought it was a male faun, for it had wide bare shoulders, and a flower-crowned head, and wore a red sarong. But then he noticed its coloring—the black hair, the bronzed skin—and realized that this was a human boy, a boy of some sixteen or seventeen years, barefoot and bare-chested.

"Kim!" cried Dymion. "Nice to see you! We were wondering if the jungle hadn't swallowed you for good."

Kim Lee stood by his father's carved throne, and smiled. He was a well-built boy, but his muscles were smoothed over and graceful—his shape seemed almost to flow. He had the family's high cheekbones, and strange eyes, and his smile had a curious twist to it.

"I've been out talking to the plants," he said.

Rosina now acted the polite hostess, and made the necessary introductions. "Helen you know already, of course."

"Hi, Kim," said Helen. She had not taken her eyes off the boy since he had come in.

"Helen . . ." said Kim, looking long at her. Then he turned to his father; but Lucius spoke first.

"What food did you eat in the forest, Kimon?"

"Oh, I took a satchel, and some biscuits," said the boy. "Imagine, Father! I fed a biscuit to old Two-Lips, and she took it!"

"Took it? How?" said Lucius.

"Between the lips. Swallowed—gone!" Kim yawned, and stretched. He wandered over to Helen's couch, touched the girl lightly on the shoulder, and lay down beside her. He then took a grape from the basket on the table before them and ate it calmly and slowly.

"Pardon me," said Mark. "What's Old Two-Lips?"

"Pardon *me,"* said Lucius abruptly, and rose from his seat, and hurriedly left the room.

No one seemed particularly surprised at this exit. So Mark repeated his question:

"What's this Two-Lips?"

Kim did not bother to reply. He was fondling Helen, and Helen was caressing him eagerly.

"I think we might as well retire now," said Rosina hurriedly, rising from her couch. "You'll all be tired after your journey, and it's getting late. Mark, Meriam, let me wish you a very good night."

As they went out—all, that is, but Kim and Helen, who were still stretched on their couch, oblivious—Mark in desperation caught Rosina by the arm.

"Do you know what this Two-Lips is, Mistress Lee?"

"Oh," she said, "I think it's a nickname the menfolk have given to a certain plant."

"A plant?"

"Yes. A big thing, rather rare, buried deep in the jungle. I think it's one of those beetle-swallowers. I'm sorry I can't help you much, I'm not a botanist."

"Trappola," said Mark. "Maybe the species *magniflora.* At a guess. That's an insect-eater."

"Yes, very likely, something like that."

The garden was very dark as they crossed it to their

pavilion. A fine rain was falling, and the clouds were too thick to let through any moongleams. Mark reminded Meriam that none of the native Dextran snakes could harm them.

But Meriam had recovered her good spirits; in fact, she was giggling. "I don't think Helen is going to bother you much more, Mark—nor even fool around with Dymion. Did you see how she was acting with Kim Lee?"

"And he with her," said Mark. "Beautiful little savage, isn't he? But I wonder, I really wonder how he managed to persuade a Dextran plant to eat an Earthly biscuit!"

As they reached their pavilion, they found Circe and Chloe sitting on the steps. The faun girls rose to greet them.

"Good even, Maister, Mistress," they chorused. "Will ye be washing, bathing, taking a cup of hippocras, or e'en going straight to bed?"

"Straight to bed," said Meriam decidedly; and added, under her breath, "together."

Chapter Ten

When they woke, morning was bright and cool, and from afar they could hear the haunting melody of the Dextran sirenbird.

Circe and Chloe were kneeling beside their bed, smiling. Meriam blushed, and hurriedly covered herself with the sheet. Mark chuckled.

"What is it, nymphs?" he said.

"A glorious good morrow, my Maister," said Chloe.

"And store of sons to my Mistress," said Circe. "If ye have done embracing for the nonce, will ye be for bathing? The morn is sweet, and so is the river."

"Come on, darling, let's go," said Mark, springing up from the mattress as lightly as gravity allowed. He stood up on the wooden floor and stretched, fully naked. "There's no need to be coy with these girls. They're innocents."

"How do we bathe?" said Meriam, still hugging the sheet to her breast. "I'm not going swimming naked."

"We will bring cloths, my lady," said Circe.

And they did. Mark and Meriam went down to the river dressed faunlike in a couple of red sarongs, Meriam wearing hers pulled up to her shoulders. She indeed bathed in her sarong; Mark, as soon as he was in the water, discarded his and swam about naked like everybody else.

For the river was fairly thronged. Helen and Kim were there, and quite a few fauns and nymphs, and even a couple of young centaurs, both pale-brown-furred, a male and a female. The centaurs swam strongly against the current and right across the river and back several times. Helen after a while enlivened the scene by clambering on to the back of the male centaur, and was carried by him so from midstream back to the Flora bank. Her weight altogether submerged his rear body, so that she clung to his manlike torso like a mermaid embracing a mythical Triton. At last the boy-stallion shook her off in the shallows, puffing and uttering deep centaur laughter. Kim next tried the same game with the girl-centaur, but she threw him at once and took refuge beside her male.

"Faith, Maister Kimon," she spluttered, tossing her mane, "thou'st grown too ponderous and massy o' late. If thou'lt make the beast with two backs now, thou must seek out thine own kindly mate."

"Huhini's right at that," laughed Kim, and began pursuing Helen, who certainly did not try very hard to escape.

Meriam said, "Shall we be going, Mark?"

"Yes," agreed Mark. "I've better things to do than watch their antics. I want to know more about this jungle, and more about centaurs in particular. I must go and tackle Dymion."

"All right," said Meriam, "and I'd like to have a talk with Rosina."

Mark found Dymion on the *Naiad,* in company with a couple of nymphs in gaily patterned sarongs and flowers tucked behind their pointed ears. Ostensibly, all three were splicing some pieces of rope.

"She needs a bit of an overhaul," said Dymion hurriedly as Mark appeared in the rear cabin, and removed his arm from the waist of one of the green girls.

"Do you mean the ship?" said Mark.

Dymion relaxed and burst out laughing. "All right, all right. Let's not beat about the jungle thickets. Do you know, Mark, in old Earth history, about the princely rogue who once found himself head of a famous church? He said, 'Since God has given us the Papacy, let us enjoy it.' I feel much the same way about Flora. Since whatever god or goddess rules the affairs of Dextra has given me a marvelous little princedom on these shores, why shouldn't I enjoy the perks of it? The perks, as you can see, include some very pretty and obliging little girls, and I'm not fussy about their color. And there's plenty of them! Enough for you too. Are you alone for the moment?"

"Meriam's with Rosina."

"Good, good—the poor household spies can delude each other. See here, Mark, we've got these *two* ravishing wenches handy, take your pick, I can spare one. Doesn't matter which—they're much the same—"

"Er—not just now, if you don't mind, Dymion," said

Mark, faintly repulsed. "What I really came to say is—if you're not too heavily occupied—I'd like some directions to get to the nearest centaur village."

"Oh, let's make it a trip and go there together." Dymion scrambled to his feet. "I can handle these—well, ropes—many another time. It's only a morning's walk to the centaurs and back. Come on."

The village of the Wise Serpents lay upstream, northward, and an hour's journey into the forest. Dymion found a small dinghy and rowed Mark across the river. They walked for a while along the north bank, then struck off into the jungle by a well-trodden path.

The day was warming up now, and the jungle was slumbrous with heavy airs and the murmuring of native parabees. Mark noted a number of brightly colored flowers, some as much as half a meter across, but all were of species he had seen before in botanical collections in New Jerusalem. The insects, too, were not absolute surprises, though he was struck by the number of airfish—the little floating fliers of New Asia, which used not wings but enclosed sacs of hydrogen to keep them aloft in the thick atmosphere.

"Damned aerial plankton," he muttered, brushing them away from his face.

Indeed, there were larger insects preying on the airfish, and handibirds preying on the larger insects. This was a country more lush with life than any he had known before, more lush than he could have believed—and it extended south of the Serpent River, behind Midbar, all the way to Hind and the Southern Ocean, a swampy, seething, writhing mass of native living things. To talk of *clearing* it, as some of the Saints were doing! It was insanity. Of course, to the Lordists in their green-and-brown semi-desert, the mush of New Asia lay there like a succubus, an insidious menace to their whole uptight way of life. The land of Lilith.

If it came to a battle between Lilith and the Lord, whose side would *he* be on? Lilith, he thought, brushing away yet another airfish—she was a bit *much*. Pity the two forces couldn't each keep in its own land—and let some lands be a happy mixture, a medium.

They had arrived. All at once there was a wide clearing filled with short blue grass, and some patches of Dextran cereals, and small wooden buildings. The houses around the perimeter of the clearing were very like the pavilions of Flora, and of a size suitable for the centaurs' nuclear families. Beside them were kitchen sheds, from the stone chimneys of which in some cases smoke was rising. In the very center of the clearing stood a large block of black wood, and upon it what looked at first glance like an equestrian group—actually, a life-sized stone carving of a pair of centaurs, male and female, one arm around each other's waist, the other hand extended and holding a small stone disk.

"All very impressive," said Mark, "I had no idea . . ."

"It's mostly quite recent," said Dymion. "This lot were the most advanced, but even they had only flimsy shelters when we first arrived. The statue was done only last year. They've been developing terrifically fast, and they give *us* a lot of the credit. There are other tribes, you know, most of them farther north, on the edge of the great plains. And most of them are still wildish, without cereals, without fire."

The clearing was fairly well populated with centaur villagers, including, to Mark's delight, a number of little centaur foals. And now they had been spotted; and Xathax came forward to welcome them.

"Ah, fair sirs," he boomed. "Good-den to you both. You do us honor . . ."

Dymion explained that Mark was there more or less as a tourist, and he was thereupon given a conducted tour of the whole village. He was impressed by the kitchens and weaving sheds and houses, and amused by the centaurs' beds and stools. The beds were extremely wide mattresses (since centaurs normally slept on their sides), while the stools were rectangular blocks of wood. Xathax demonstrated their use by "sitting" on one—that is, he rested his rear belly on it, thus transferring his weight from his legs to his second, rear set of ribs.

The tour ended at the base of the central statue. Xathax said it represented his people's ideal—self-harmony, and reverence and gratitude for "the fruits of the forest."

"What fruits?" asked Mark, gazing up at the stone figures. "They seem to be holding little cakes."

"That is a product of the forest," said Xathax gravely. "Ah, without the forest we would not be what we are! The forest has fostered us, and Men have fathered in us discourse of reason, the noble Word, by means of which we but lately came into our own."

"What do you mean," said Mark, " 'the forest has fostered you'?"

Xathax stroked his beard. "There is wisdom in the forest, which we have tasted of. And there be some movers who have drunk more deeply. But that is not the centaurs' way. One can perhaps accept too many gifts from the Mother."

"I am not following you," said Mark.

Xathax smiled. "Should men follow centaurs? That would be strange! But, Sir Mark, mayhap I am not well practiced in your words, and mayhap that which you would learn cannot be taught in words at all. It must be tasted, chewed, digested. Which needeth time. Time! Maister Lucius has been seeking the wisdom of the forest for many years now; and will you seek to swallow it all at once?"

Mark shrugged. "I'm no mystic, Handy. Let's get back to facts. How do you live? What do you eat—is it only these cakes and vegetables? How is your tribe governed?"

Xathax told him. The centaurs were basically browsers, fruit and nut eaters, but they had lately been extending their diet by cooking a wide range of vegetable foodstuffs. At one time they had eaten meat also, but had given this up for moral reasons. Anyway, there was some especially nourishing food in this part of the forest, and they no longer missed eating meat.

As for the government of the tribe, it hardly existed. Xathax had been elected Speaker, or envoy to other tribes and rational species, but he was not a chief. All important decisions were taken by the tribe collectively.

"What happens if you have different opinions?" asked Mark. "Do you argue? Do you vote?"

Xathax smiled. "No. We never need to argue. We share our feelings. Not as much as do the fauns—but we still share."

"You see?" said Dymion. "That old witchcraft again."

As they came away, Mark said, "Well, there's one thing I'm relieved about. They *do* speak among themselves. I heard some of the children playing together. Their own language, too. Fancy them claiming they only developed it in the last four hundred years."

It was even hotter walking back through the jungle, hot and humid. Dymion said, "I reckon we'll be getting the full monsoon in a few days. It's due."

They plodded on in silence for a while, Mark swatting the occasional airfish. Dymion led the way at first, then fell back, puffing.

"I'm not in the best of condition, I suppose. Let's take it easy. Besides, Mark—there's something I want to put to you." He paused. "I had a few words with my father yesterday, before dinner. You know, he likes you a lot."

"He has funny ways of showing it. What does he mean by calling me a 'quester'?"

"Well, you *are* on a sort of a quest, aren't you? Trying to track down the mystery of the fauns. Good luck to you on that, but I prefer just to enjoy them! Look, don't be put off by my father's odd manner. Once you get to know him better . . . But that's the point I want to make. See here, Mark: how do you like Flora?"

"Magnificent. I liked Classica, too, but this is overwhelming! Atlantis plus. I wish I could stay here longer. You can't imagine how I regret losing nine years of my life to a Puritan dump like Livya."

"Then why go back?" said Dymion.

"What?"

"Why go back? We could pass a message via Sunion's radio on my next trip—tell your Agency, your university, that you've resigned. And your girl Meriam too, of course. Better pretend you're settling in Classica, we want to keep Flora out of the limelight. Then, Mark, you can join the stead here as a partner. An honorary Lee."

"Did your father propose that?" said Mark.

"Not exactly—he's cryptic, even with me. But I'm sure he'd be happy—and he's only nominally the steader now, you know; Rosina and I run things. Mark, this is going to be a great, a magnificent country one day, an empire of fauns and centaurs, if they and we can keep the Saints at bay. And the native creatures are so friendly, we could live like real princes here. Found a human colony, separate from the rest of the world, *independent* as my father says. We wouldn't be a First Hundred, but we'd be a first six or seven—three breeding couples, since I don't think Helen will be going back. We could raise our kids here—to hell with radio school! We'll be our own school."

"Have you talked this over with Rosina?" asked Mark.

"No, but—"

"Well, I could talk it over with Meriam," said Mark, "but I'm sure her answer would be no."

"That would depend on how you went about it," said Dymion, looking sly. "I expect I'll have some problems with Rosina, too. Best not to spring it on them too abruptly."

"I would have a worse problem. I'd have to go back to Livya at least for a while—Meriam wants to be married there, respectably."

"Oh, why bother with such formalities?" said Dymion. "I'm sure Helen and Kim won't. Besides, you might like to leave things flexible."

"No, no," said Mark, suddenly irritated. "That won't do at all! Dymion, I *love* Meriam. This is really a crazy scheme, you know."

"Look," said Dymion, coming to a momentary halt. "You don't have to decide about it now. Mull it over, Mark. I think you'll come to realize you have a lot in common with us here. Why go slaving away for years in Livya? You don't have any loyalty to Livya! Or their narrow traditions. Here we can make our own traditions, live like pashas . . ."

They trudged on in silence. Mark had read up just enough Earth history to know how pashas were reputed to have lived.

He guessed he knew what Dymion's scheme meant. It meant having little green girls in bed whenever you felt like it. Dozens of little Chloes as concubines.

Dammit, he couldn't help being tempted by the idea. No man could. And his loyalty to Livya—that was certainly nonexistent.

But his loyalty to Meriam? That was something else again. Pity the Chloes and Meriam weren't compatible.

But they weren't—he knew Meriam quite well enough now to be sure of that. And he knew which he preferred.

They were just in time for lunch at Flora, which today involved only the four of them—Dymion, Rosina, Mark, Meriam. Conversation during the meal was mainly about preparations for the evening's feast. Afterward, when they had returned to their pavilion and were alone, Mark and Meriam compared notes.

"I've been loafing about the stead," said Meriam, "chatting with Rosina, and also with the faun maids. Mark, my dear, I don't know what to say first! Circe told me Lucius has not been around since yesterday evening—he went off upriver just after dinner last night. And Helen and Kim have vanished into the forest. As for Dymion—well, you were with him, but—I've learned a few things about his character. Circe—to put it bluntly, Circe says that Dymion once 'lay with her.' That seems to be his chief recreation, now, since these greenskin fauns showed up at Flora six months ago."

"I believe you—he does seem to have a touch of satyriasis. Did Circe tell you where the greenies were *before* six months ago? I've never managed to get anything useful on that from any faun—they always just say 'in the forest.' "

"Well, yes, they said that, our two girls," Meriam mused. "Chloe also said, 'We were different, before.' "

"Different." Mark savored the word. Then a thought struck him. "O Lord, Meri—have you noticed—around this stead there *aren't any faun children!*"

"Not yet, no. But there will be. Mark—Circe says she's two months pregnant."

"By whom? No! That's not possible!"

"No, it's not, is it? Frankly, Circe wasn't sure, but she *thinks* the father could be a boy faun."

And then Mark licked his lips and said, "Meri, Dymion wants us both to stay here—for good."

Meriam's reaction was exactly what he had expected.

The Fourth of July festival was held not in the house but in a nearby open space, a large lawn of mingled green and blue grass, half Earthly and half Dextran. Around the lawn were beds of similarly mixed flowers, and behind these, as a fringe before the forest, a planted hedgerow of young green and purple trees.

"We call it Concord," said Rosina, as the al fresco feast was beginning. "Dymion and I did the spadework, four years ago—with local help, of course." She nodded at the centaur guests and the faun servants. "It was Lucius' idea—he wanted it to be a meeting place, to symbolize mingling. But maybe mingling can be carried too far—in some directions."

Dymion was some way off, having his cup filled by a young faun. There were vine leaves in his hair, and he wore only a loose purple robe; with his free hand he was caressing one of the nymph maids. Mark guessed he had been sampling the wine before the party had officially begun.

"Where is everybody?" said Meriam hurriedly. "No sign of Lucius yet?"

"No," said Rosina. "Well, he's often been off on trips upcountry before. As for Helen and Kim—they're back. When last heard of, they were bathing again. Ah—here they are."

Helen and Kim arrived arm in arm, from the direction of the river. Both were dressed exactly alike, in red sarongs which covered them only from the waist down, and they wore flowers in their hair and behind their ears.

Meriam blushed crimson. "Fancy her coming like *that!*" she whispered.

"Perhaps this is going to be one of Dymion's New Traditions," said Mark, smiling. "The new style for ladies of Flora."

He did not say so, but really he thought Helen looked

very pretty. The mode suited her. A golden-skinned, golden-haired nymph . . .

The party began to go well. After the meats and fruits had mostly been cleared, some of the faun-boys and nymph-girls sat down among the guests as feasters themselves, and filled their cups with native Dextran wine. Helen amiably caressed a faun-boy, but getting no useful response from him, turned her attentions back to Kim. Xathax and the other centaurs knelt on the grass somewhat apart, sipping their wine and observing the antics of the other supposedly rational creatures like four-legged philosophers. The sun was setting.

Dymion wandered over and sat down near Mark, Meriam and Rosina.

"Lovely evening," he said a trifle thickly. "All we need now is for some wood god to come to us out of the forest. Pan, or Dionysus . . . Ah, here *does* come somebody, right on cue. But dammit, it's only my father."

"No, he's got a retinue," said Rosina. "What are *those?*"

Lucius stepped out of the shadowy hedgerow accompanied by eight human-sized figures.

It was that point of evening when colors are most vivid. At first Mark thought that Lucius' companions were naked men and women; then, as the warm late light caught their faces, he realized that they were fauns and nymphs—four of each, but tall as humans, and brightly golden skinned. No mere suntan: they seemed to be gilded. Their faces were quite beautiful, with expressions of unearthly calm; their lips were red, their ears rounded, their hair a shimmering green.

"Ye *gods!*" gasped Dymion, "the ultimate—!"

Mark gripped Meriam's hand. "Oh no," he breathed. "Not another species!"

"Darling," said Meriam, "you were expecting them, really, weren't you? The superfauns."

"These have to be the last," said Mark, staring, fascinated. "They've reached the height limit. And—they're no longer fauns and nymphs—they're gods and goddesses!"

The "gods" came forward, and bowed to Dymion and Rosina. One of the gold-skinned males addressed Dymion:

"Good even, Sir Captain. Great thanks, once again, for transporting us back to the land of the Mother. As thou seest, we are much the better for it."

"Who *are* you?" cried Dymion.

"Call me Silvanus," said the golden one. "It comes to me now, so the Mother teaches me, that this—" he touched his chest—"was once the body of Springol, but methinks that name suits no longer with this present quality."

"And this was Topsy," said a golden goddess, "now better called Terpsichore."

"And this is Melpomene," said another, "for I have put off the old Mopsa."

"Oh, *no!*" groaned Mark. "Not our former shipmates—those ugly little blue half-hairies!"

"Thou hast said it, human," agreed Silvanus, with dignity. "We are indeed the perfection of faundom—after us comes none other. Dymion, when we are all well rested, and thou art ready and thy bark yare for another voyage, we will be pleased to company with thee again: for indeed, we are bound for Classica."

"I need another drink," said Dymion.

"And so do I," said Lucius loudly.

The old man was standing in the midst of the feasters, encircled at a little distance by fauns and centaurs. He was holding a purple-painted wine jar. From this he poured into a cup, put down the jar, and raised the cup high.

"I give you humans all a toast," he said. "Independence! This you see now before you, achieved, accomplished."

And he tossed back the cup, and drank it off.

"That's *wild* wine," whispered Meriam, gripping Mark's arm. "I wish he wouldn't show off like that. He'll be sick."

But Lucius seemed to relish his wine. He poured himself another cup, and drank from it, savoring it now, sipping slowly.

"Endymion, Kimon," he said, "my sons, congratulate me. I have found that which I was seeking all those years. Total union, total communion. I am in Her, and She in me."

"Really, father?" said Dymion. "That's going a bit far, no? Even I wouldn't want to do that. I don't mind swallowing—" he took a gulp of his own wine—"but I do object to being swallowed."

"I am not swallowed," said Lucius, "or, if I was swallowed, I was delivered, born again. It was my fear, my reluctant fear that led me to dream of Her, all those years ago, in such a terrifying shape. Now I know that she is not dreadful, but loving. She has given me true Independence—not as she gives to fauns, but to centaurs. I am still a Man."

"Mark, I don't like this," said Meriam suddenly. "I'm frightened. Will you take me home now?"

"Home?" said Mark. "That's not so easy. Home is a long way. But to the pavilion—yes, yes . . ."

They stole away into the darkness. Behind them, the noise of the reveling continued.

Chapter Eleven

The next morning dawned dark, hot, with low clouds and a hint of thunder. Mark woke up with a hangover. There were no nymph maids about.

He left Meriam sleeping, got up, found his notes, and added at the bottom of his table of fauns:

Species	*Date of Discovery*	*Average Height* (cm)	*Brain Capacity* (cc)
aureus* ("Goldskin")	7.4.514	c. 165	1400** ?

Meriam opened her eyes and said, "Husband."

Mark knelt and kissed her. "Yes, darling?"

"What are we going to do? About—everything?"

Mark passed his hand across his brow, wiping off a drop of sweat. "If Dymion does make another voyage to Classica soon, and if he'll take us, I vote we go with him. But that can't be for two or three days at least. The *Naiad* needs a bit of overhauling, and he'd have to lay in stores. Meanwhile—I want to get to the bottom of this mystery."

"How?"

"Tackle Lucius. I think he knows everything, and he may be willing to talk. And—I want to go into the jungle, upriver. See where those transformed fauns came from. Do you realize, darling, if they really *were* transformed from blueskins to goldskins, what would be entailed? Something like the metamorphosis of an insect, but in a *mammal.* Plus a gross increase in body substance—they would have doubled their body weight in *twenty-four hours!* It's crazy, impossible, beyond anything our applied biologists could do. Maybe Lucius is a genius, has some kind of superfactory. Whatever it is, it can't be far—not more than a few hours' journey at the most."

"Mark, aren't you scared—of going into that jungle?"

"Frankly, yes—a bit. Well, more than a bit. But I must. It's where this whole trip has led me. I can't let go now—I have to know."

"Well, if you're going," said Meriam, "then so am I."

"What? There's no need—"

"Yes there is need," she said. "I've done enough sociology in Classica and here to fill all the books I shall ever write, and in fact I'm quite tired of my *informants.* Do you expect me to hang around here talking to Rosina and Dymion and the fauns while you. . . . Mark, to be honest, I'm scared stiff—for both of us. You know it's not just a *factory!* Not from the way Lucius talked. There's something dreadful, unnatural, monstrous in this forest, and you know it. Well, if you're going into danger, I'm going with you."

"I tell you there's no need," he said. "I shouldn't allow it."

"Who are you to *allow?"* Meriam looked almost ferocious. "I'm glad the Sifters threw out all that rot in the Old Scriptures about wives *obeying* husbands! That's not going to be the way of it between us, Mark. Side by side, it has to be. Anyway, Mark—do you think I'd really be quite safe *here,* without you? When we don't know *what's* going on?"

There was a silence. Finally, Mark nodded.

"All right, if you feel that way about it."

"I do."

They washed, and as though preparing for battle put

on their Agency uniforms, and Mark his sandals and Meriam her boots, and both went out to find Lucius.

The old man's pavilion at the back of the house seemed to be surrounded by fauns. On the wooden steps the eight new godlike goldskins were being silently admired by a large crowd of green males and females—apparently all the house servants.

"Where's Lucius?" said Mark loudly.

Springol-Silvanus raised his lordly head. "Within," he said superciliously.

And then the door opened, and Lucius stood framed in the doorway.

"Ah, the seekers," he said, smiling. "Come in, both of you."

They threaded their way through the crowd of fauns, past the naked golden gods, and followed Lucius into his den. It was a large dark room with a darker inner doorway leading presumably to a bedchamber. There were shelves of books, a desk, strange-looking diagrams and pictures of gods and mythical beasts affixed to the walls. Also a chair and two stools.

"Sit," said Lucius, indicating the stools and taking the chair himself.

"You seem to be expecting us," said Mark.

"I have been expecting you a long time. And not only I. All right: now ask what you are going to ask."

"I'll come straight to the point," said Mark. "What is it that keeps turning out new types of fauns?"

"Do you think I know the answer to that question?"

"Yes, I do."

Lucius chuckled. "You are right. Far be it from me to deny Her gifts!" He paused, and looked at them both. "Yes, I know. But if I told you, you would not believe me. So I won't tell you. Not yet. Not—here."

"Where then?" said Meriam.

"Where She abides. Up the river, and in the forest."

He rose. "When you have seen, then you may believe. And then we can talk profitably about Her. I am ready to go to Her now. Are you?"

"Well," said Meriam, "we haven't had breakfast yet."

"It is indeed better to go fasting. In fasting and recollection . . . and it is only two hours' march. Less."

Mark rose. "All right. But I have to go back to my room first."

Lucius smiled. "By all means, bring that pistol. It will not be required; but if it makes you any happier . . ."

There was no stable of hexips at Flora, so the three of them had to walk along the bank of the Serpent River, up past the crossing to the centaurs' village. They did not pass any fauns or centaurs or humans. The world of Anthis seemed deserted. Even the birds were unusually silent.

For an elderly man, Lucius seemed remarkably spry; it was all the young people could do to keep up with him, and they were soon sweating. Mark said as much, and complimented Lucius.

"It's clean living that does it, my boy," replied the old man. "I am no roisterer; I took no more wine last night than you saw me drink on that very special occasion. And I do not waste my substance in other ways—I cannot afford to live like my son Endymion. A true seeker for mental power must be chaste. You might do well to remember that yourselves."

Mark looked at Meriam. She had reddened; on the other hand, she might be merely flushed with the heat.

It grew even hotter, especially when they turned away from the river and struck south along a broad trail which led into the heart of the jungle. Here the air was laden with bittersweet scents. The airfish floated thickly. And then Mark noticed something else.

"What are these?" he said, trying to pluck a floating

ball out of the air. It was about two centimeters across, like a small soap bubble, with dandelionlike hairs. It eluded his hand. A few others drifted across the path.

Lucius looked, and said, "Seeds."

"Oh," said Mark. "Oh, yes, I remember. Some genera of the octofungi have these floating spores. Like airfish, they're filled with light-gas pockets. That way, they can drift for kilometers."

"What are octofungi?" said Meriam. "I've heard the term before, but I'm not too clear."

"They are really strange creatures," said Mark. "You know how in the sea there are many things that look like plants, but are really animals? Like the Earthly anemones. Have roots, but will travel. Well, here on Dextra—at least in New Asia—you find some *land* creatures like that. People often call them plants—even I do when I'm not talking to biologists—but strictly they're animals—animals which have adopted a plantlike way of life. They're distantly related, believe it or not, to the Dextran vertebrates. They share the same origin in the sea—the octobrachs. But while the vertebrates developed a fore-and-aft body and six limbs, the octofungi kept their radial symmetry, and began anchoring themselves. One group—the octofung*oids*—those developed cyanophyll, and went in for photosynthesis, and so became very nearly real plants! But others did not. *Trappola* is one of those—an insect-eater. It has aerial spores, rather like those." He frowned. "But I don't think those can be spores of even the largest *Trappola*. They're about four times too big."

Lucius raised his hand. "Now, hush. No more words. We are approaching."

He led them forward along the path, which was widening, almost on tiptoes. The jungle was utterly silent, except for a faint strange humming, barely audible.

Then Lucius stepped aside, and motioned them forward, past him. Light increased: a clearing. Mark and

Meriam stood on the edge of the black-trunked trees, hand in hand, peering.

At first Mark could not interpret the strange shapes that filled the middle of the clearing. In the very center was a great pinkish sphere two or three meters in diameter, half buried in the soil so that its top rose only to shoulder level. From this great sphere, huge plantlike structures projected right, left and toward the humans. Some were tubes like horizontal tree trunks propped half a meter above ground, presumably by roots, and surrounded by blue circular leaves. Others were massive projections about the size and shape of stranded rowboats, their "sterns" fixed to a fleshy collar round the central sphere; the pointed ends of the "boats" were curled downward to the ground like enormous flower petals, and terminated in long tendrils or tentacles well over two meters long and as thick as a man's arm.

"What is it?" whispered Meriam. "Mark, it's *huge!*"

"An octofungoid, I guess," said Mark, staring, "but no known species. No known genus. Ten times as big as a *Trappola!* My Lord . . ."

Lucius said, hissing: "Name not your foreign Lord! This is She. In one of her flowerings. Fear not: she is benign. You may approach."

Mark did not want to approach—not yet. He felt his laser, checking that it slid easily in its holster, and studied the animal-plant. Yes—certainly on octofungoid: there were just *four* of those boat-sized petals, arranged crosswise, alternating with another cross, the four leaf-bearing arms. It was reassuring that She had blue leaves! That implied photosynthesis, not . . .

As he watched, a large beetle sailed across the clearing, coming from a wide pathway beyond. The insect must have been ten centimeters long, and more in wingspread. It moved straight across and down, down to the top center of the great pink sphere . . . and was gone.

Then Mark knew what Kim had meant by "Old Two-Lips." The top of the sphere had two liplike structures, half a meter long, and purplish. These lips opened as quickly as though they were a giant human mouth, and tiny red tendrils shot upwards, enclosing the doomed beetle in a living cage of tongues. Then the tongues slipped into the sphere, the lips closed.

And the humming sound was louder. The purple lips were slightly blurred, vibrating. Mmmmmmmm . . .

"How nice it smells here," said Meriam. "Doesn't it, Lucius?"

Lucius did not reply. He had gone forward, and now he was bending over a projection of the Plant, one of the leaf-stem ends. This was a large terminal leaf bearing what looked like small cakes—disk-shaped knobs on the upper surface.

Mark was having trouble focusing his thoughts. Yes, Meri was right: there *was* a lovely perfume in the grove. What was Lucius doing? He was plucking off a disk, eating fruit-cake. Fruit of the Plant, of Her body. How clever of him, to eat native food.

And now Lucius was going away, fading out of the clearing, out of the scene altogether. Oh well: forget him. It was really too hot to think about anything but immediate impressions.

He began unbuttoning his clothes. This was only reasonable: too hot, too hot . . . Meriam was stripping, too.

My sister, my spouse. How beautiful she was!

"Mark," said Meriam, clinging to him, naked. "What a good place this is. Let's make love."

"Yes," he said, "yes."

They walked toward the Plant. Must find a good place. This was all a Good Place, but one spot was more appropriate, more fitting. Of course, a boat-petal . . .

Inside, the petal was more like a bath. It was all purple-pink, and there were little holes along the bottom. A leaky ship . . . and the ship was filling, leaking, but leaking perfume, the holes were emitting fragrance, nard and myrrh for the nuptial bed, the nuptial bath, the nuptial ball—for the place was no longer a boat, the vessel was spherical, they were lying in a hollow sphere, a womb-tomb, enveloped in sweetness.

Meriam's body, a girl's body, seemed to envelop him too. The Queen had brought him into her chambers. She was all sweetness, a bundle of myrrh, a lily of the valley, rose of Sharon, a garden enclosed, a fountain sealed up, her locks wet with dew . . . honeydew . . .

What a lovely dream. He was being turned over, over-turned, mobilized, Möbius-stripped, outside turning in-side, hisness becoming herness, his sinister places her righteousness. He, Mark, was being saved, salved, made whole by her holes . . . and vice versa. He was becoming Meriam. The Turners were turning into each other . . .

What a lovely dream. She was being turned over, over-turned, her holeness made his wholeness, wholly holy, her wholly of whollies filled with dew, and the King had brought himself into her chambers, she was marked with his Mark, she was Mark . . . his left hand was away from her, his right hand did embrace her . . .

He was coming into his own now, but not only. He was still holy, wholly . . . how interesting, how beautiful to be now-and-ever-shall-be in part a woman! He-she, Mark-Meriam, was walking hand in hand, right hand in left hand. The Lady said unto my Lady, sit down at my left-right hand until I make thine enemy thy friend . . . and my Lord-Lady, his-her locks are wet with dew in-deed, we are wet all over, all through. And he-she goeth in unto me. I am gone into, I am taken, my bowels are moved. And something is being *re*-moved . . . improved. All for my own good, for his good, for her good, his-her-our good. Good . . .

The two young people lay side by side, naked, pleasantly cool. The boat-bed was comfortable. Better than a mattress . . .

Mark stirred. He looked at Meriam, whose eyes were fluttering.

"Where are we?" he said.

Memory came back. "Meriam!" he cried.

Meriam sat up. "What—what? Mark! I had such a strange dream . . ."

He sighed with relief. "Thank the Lord—you're all right. Aren't you?"

"Yes. I was only asleep."

"So was I." He looked about: the clearing seemed comfortable, homely, not at all frightening. They were in a petal of the Plant, and the Plant was friendly. That was nice. But they would have to go now, back home. Flora was home, their pavilion. "We'd better get dressed," he said.

Meriam gave him her hand, and gaily he pulled her out of the huge petal. How nice to be naked in this friendly clearing. Pity to have to put on those tight uniforms, now—but there was some reason for that, which it was still hard to remember. Well, what must be, must be.

They were buttoning each other's jackets when Lucius appeared from the shadows. He looked at them, then came forward and embraced them, one after the other.

"I see you are all *right,"* he said.

"Why, yes," said Mark. "Never felt more right in all my life."

"Good. Have you eaten of the Fruit yet?" He indicated the knob-disks on the leaf-arm of the Plant.

"No," said Meriam, shaking her head as if to clear it. "We can't—I remember now—that's native food. It wouldn't agree with us."

"You'd be surprised," said Lucius.

"No," said Mark, "Meriam's right. We'd better be getting along home now."

Lucius looked at them for a long moment, then shrugged. "All right," he said. "I suppose you need time to get used to it. Come on, then."

When they got back to Flora, it was late afternoon. Almost time for dinner. The journey through the jungle and downriver had passed like a dream.

"We must have slept for quite a while," said Meriam. "Crazy thing to do, going to sleep in a plant! And I felt confused for a long time afterward."

It was only when Lucius had taken leave of them that they remembered—remembered that they had not asked him, finally, about the transformer of the fauns.

"Oh well," said Mark, as they washed in the pavilion, "we'll ask him at dinner. And maybe go back to the forest tomorrow. Somehow, I don't feel afraid of the jungle any more."

"Nor do I," said Meriam. "Mark, I don't feel afraid of *anything!*"

"Fine, darling, fine. But I'm hungry. Come on."

After the disturbances of the Independence Feast, Flora seemed to be coming back to normal. The gold-skinned superfauns were no longer about, and the green house servants were back at their duties.

"The gods have vanished," said Rosina, as they assembled in the dining room. "Gone back into the forest. I hope they stay there." And she looked coldly at Dymion, who seemed rather the worse for wear physically, but in very good spirits.

"My lady, your pardon," said Dymion, half singing. "*Perdóno, perdóno*. But the best way to get rid of temptation, you know . . . I have been in Olympus, yes, much of last night; this afternoon, too. But the sword wears out the sheath, and all that. Those goddesses are . . . tiring. Rosina, my countess, from now on I shall be a reformed character, faithful—in my fashion, and at least till the next opera. Meriam, my sweet, you look ravishing."

Meriam was wearing a loose violet-colored gown. Mark too thought she looked ravishing. He beamed; she beamed. All the world was in love, people no longer had hard edges. How nice not to be jealous or uptight any more! Mark was glad he himself had come to dinner in a robe of local red cloth, not his uniform. And Helen and Kim on the next couch, both in sarongs (though Helen's pulled up a little higher): both very fetching. Kim, it seemed, had also been in Olympus, and neither Kim nor Helen were worried: they too had returned to being faithful to each other—in their fashion.

Now the servants entered, bringing in wine and fruit; and with them came Lucius, that wise old wizard. The old man was jovial.

"I shall be master of *this* feast," he said. "A family occasion, and for once I play my part as head of the family. Waiters!"

Under his directions the fauns placed green wine jars on Dymion's and Kim's tables; but a purple-painted one on his own, and another purple one before Mark and Meriam. There were two sorts of fruit being served, too, it seemed.

"Your right good health," said Lucius, raising his cup and pledging Mark and Meriam.

Everyone drank. Mark thought he had never tasted such nectar. But he now realized just how hungry he was, and tore into his fruit. It was really delicious. Ah, good, and now they were bringing in the main course . . . nut cakes, fine Floran bread, rich purple paramarrows . . .

Mark gradually became aware that Helen was staring at him and Meriam, open-mouthed.

"What's the matter?" he asked amiably.

Kim too was frowning. "Hey, you two, what are you playing at?"

Helen said, "How did you like your golden apples?"

"Fine," said Meriam, "just fine. They're better than the best oranges I ever—"

"Fairy food," said Helen, "fairy food! Are you crazy—like Lucius?"

And then Mark realized what he and his dear love had been doing. They had been drinking wild wine, and eating native Dextran food, and *liking* them!

The stuff was doing him good, too: he could feel the warm inner glow that comes from gratified digestion.

"What—what is this?" he said, surprised. "Lucius, what's going on? Are we hypnotized, or what?"

"Hypnotized? Not now," said Lucius smiling. "No, it's no illusion. Rejoice, both of you. You are the first Dextran-human pair. A new Adam and Eve, if you will. You are free. Independent. Converted. No longer invaders—but natives."

Mark sat up very straight on his couch. "If you're saying what I think you're saying, Lucius, let *me* say that's utterly impossible! That operation was tackled once, by Newstone of Landing City—the greatest biochemist this planet has ever seen. He tried biochemical conversion the other way, of course—from Dextran to Earth-type proteins, and in micro-organisms. He got nowhere. Not even after he had accepted that he'd have to kill the organisms first. It was a clear impossibility."

"With Her," said Lucius, "all things are possible."

"What, *her?*" said Kim. "You mean, old Two-Lips has swallowed Mark and Meri and spat them out again turned around, gone native?"

"Not swallowed into her mouth," said Lucius, "but taken unto herself, yes. As she takes the fauns unto herself, her children into her wombs, and returns them refurbished, improved. As she will improve *all* of you, my children, if you go to her with the right longing in your hearts."

Helen and Kim exchanged glances; then they both scrambled up, and left the room almost running.

Rosina sat upright, and said, "Lucius, this has gone too far. If this isn't a joke—"

"It is no joke. You can all become true natives if you wish it. It is not dangerous: I, Mark, and Meriam—we three are the living proof of that. I went first, and I was changed. My body was bathed through and through with Her marvel-working fluids; and since yesterday I have eaten nothing but native Dextran food and drunk nothing but native Dextran drink. They taste very good—do they not, you two?"

Meriam nodded. Mark stared, silent.

"But there is better food yet, which while you were in Her presence this day, you refused. If you eat of Her fruit, her bread, then you will have the full understanding, the mental speech, the union."

Meriam said softly, "I don't want to become a faun-girl, Lucius. I'm a human girl, and I want to stay that way."

"I've said before that there is no such danger. The centaurs eat of that bread, which gives them wisdom. As for the fauns—to understand their history, you will have to speak to their Mother Herself."

"Speak to a *plant?*" said Mark. "An octofungoid?"

"You will see," said Lucius. "It is the only way. Now, *I* have spoken enough." And he rose, and went out.

Dymion said: "Congratulations, you two. Adam and Eve! Well, Mark, you'll have to look to your wife—the green faun boys and the gold gods may fancy her now. Since she's now flesh of their flesh, they may find her appetizing, while you roam the continent of Dextra."

Meriam almost wailed. "But—but that's what so awful! I mean, we're cut off! We can't go *home!*"

"I would have thought you *were* home," said Dymion. "The whole wide planet is your home now."

"I don't want it," cried Meriam. "Why should this have happened to *us?* We're not wild! Helen might love it—I don't. I don't want to prance around with fauns and centaurs. That's all right for a holiday, but—forever! All your life! No—"

"Come, Meri," said Mark, "it's not so bad as all that. We could live in Classica—in Atlantis—anywhere where there's a supply of both kinds of food. We could make some excuse, give up our Agency jobs in New Jay, fix it somehow. We'd have to be cautious, of course, not to be found out. But we could do it."

"You could stay here," said Dymion. "Join our stead. I hereby offer you partnership in Flora. Mark, you shall be my trusty vizier, and Meriam, you'll be the sweetest of the native girls, the only black-haired goddess among all those green-haired ones."

"No," said Meriam, almost weeping. "I don't want that; and I don't want to skulk about the world either, like a criminal. I want to go home!"

Rosina left her couch, came over, and caressed her. "In that case, my dear, you'd better go back to that famous Plant, and get in touch with her, and ask her to change you back the way you were before. You never know, it might work."

"All right," said Mark. "We'll do just that—tomorrow."

Chapter Twelve

They walked back to their pavilion through great darkness and a steady rain. They did not hurry: the rain was warm. Meriam's gown and Mark's robe were soaked; but it didn't matter.

Meriam hugged him. "Darling, even if we have to stay—as we are—I'll still have you."

At the pavilion entrance sat Circe and Chloe. As the two humans approached, they rose. And Circe put her arms round Meriam.

"Lady—you are one of us now," she said. "Be not afraid, we will care for you."

"My lord Mark," said Chloe, "my brother . . ."

"Make sure he stays only your *brother,"* said Meriam, raising a smile. "So you know what's happened to us?"

"Yes, Mistress," said Circe. "You are of our family now in the Mother. And you are going back to her tomorrow. We will come with you."

Mark said, "You know a hell of a lot, you little green witches. Hey, how is it you haven't all 'gone to the Mother' already, to be changed into golden gods?"

Chloe said sadly, "We have not been called. And now the Mother has taken the Golden Ones away from us."

"I'm glad," said Meriam unexpectedly. "I like you a lot better than those Golden Ones. I'm not fond of heathen gods—fauns and nymphs are nicer. If I have to live as a nymph, among you, maybe I could put up with it. But those lordly gods—I thought they were insufferable. I liked them better when they were our little hairy shipmates. If the Mother can change people to that extent —well, I'm glad she didn't interfere with *us* much more."

"We will undress you now," said Circe.

Meriam was past being merely prudish. She stood there frankly in the lamplight of the wooden room, while Circe took off her wet gown and waistcloth. Meanwhile, Mark had peeled off his dripping robe, and given it to Chloe. Suddenly Meriam uttered a cry.

"Mark—you have no Scar! Look at your middle!"

"Look at yours," said Mark.

Meriam's slim waist was quite unmarked above the navel. The girl now smoothed her fingers over her pale clear skin from her hips to her breasts.

"O Heaven, Mark," she said. "I hope She didn't make any more *important* changes—inside! I do feel a bit different!"

Mark laughed. "Well, you *look* all right! Never so beautiful . . . and I feel quite male, where it matters, if anything more so. As for you—we'll soon find out, won't we?"

And when the green girls had extinguished the lamps, and gone out, and they were alone, the human pair were soon reassured. Meriam gave Mark full proof of her joyous femininity.

"This is a historic occasion," said Mark, kissing her, as they relaxed in one another's arms. "We are the first native-Dextran-human lovers. Nice, isn't it?"

The next morning dawned surprisingly cool and miraculously clear. Mark woke to find Meriam already up, kneeling on their mattress, and shaking him.

"Mark, Mark! Come and look! The sun . . ."

He scrambled up, and they both went out naked to the east doorway of the pavilion.

Over the purple forest, below the veil of cirrus, gleamed a broad band of clear blue sky: and in the middle of that band shone the blinding yellow disk of Delta Pavonis, the star that was Dextra's sun.

"Can you imagine," whispered Meriam, "can you imagine living on a world where that could happen *any day?* It'd be like standing always in the eye of God."

Mark turned his head aside. "It's blinding," he said.

Then the sun reached the edge of the cirrus, and the unbearable glory faded to the light of common day.

"And to think they were *used* to that—those old Earthlies," said Meriam. "How is it they weren't all mystics, all philosophers? And the First Hundred—I suppose *they* could stand that too. We—we must have changed, over those centuries."

Any doubts they might have harbored as to their biochemical status, any feeling that the events of yesterday might have been no more than a vivid dream, were soon dispelled that morning.

Little things: they went down to bathe in the river, among the green fauns, and they felt no strangeness between them and the small blue-haired people. Mark and Meriam bathed naked now, and splashed about among the small folk, and were not ashamed.

For that matter, Mark had an odd sensation of *blurring*—he felt not entirely separate from the water in which he was swimming, nor entirely separate from the other living creatures about him—the splashing fauns, the singing handibirds. When a purple-feathered bird snapped up a beetle on the wing, he could almost feel his own teeth crunch on chitin, his own skin shatter in the jaws of death. He realized now that this blurring, this participation, had been growing in him ever since they had returned from the forest the previous day. It was now unmistakable—but not overpowering: he could, when he felt like it, withdraw his attention from the brother-and-sisterhood of Dextra; on the other hand, the potentiality was always here, waiting on the edges of his consciousness, available if and when he wanted it.

It did not amount to clear telepathy. But for Mark the best thing of all was this, that he was now very close to Meriam—closer than close—inside. He knew now how it felt to *be* Meriam: to have Mark Turner for a lover; and to be admired now by quite a few boy-fauns on the banks of that river.

"Well, let them admire me—her," he said to himself: for he felt also the goodwill of the fauns, their tact and real friendliness. How curiously wrong the old myths were: these half-human children of the forest were no savage rapists. For that matter, neither were the centaurs.

Being of one substance with Dextra had also its negative side, though. As they walked back to their pavilion, both Mark and Meriam had to brush away several little native stinging flies.

"We smell right to them now," said Mark, "in fact, we're edible. The forest may be more dangerous for us today. Remind me to bring my laser when we go. And we'd better wear our uniforms; they'll help keep off the insects."

Chloe and Circe shared breakfast with them in the pavilion—Dextran bread, and golden apples. Both the bread and the fruit tasted very good.

When they had finished eating, they made their preparations. As they were going out, on the steps of the pavilion they met Lucius and Dymion and Rosina.

"If you're ready," said Rosina seriously, "we'd like to go to the forest with you—all of us."

They had not gone far up the riverside path when they found two centaurs waiting for them: Xathax and his wife Xilifil.

"We were ware of your errand," boomed Xathax, "and, Sir Mark, Lady Meriam, we would be blithe to accompany you. It may be that the Mother of the Forest will have somewhat to say also to centaurs; and I may speak for and to my tribe."

The party thus became almost a procession—five humans, two centaurs, and the nymphs Chloe and Circe. After a while, the centaurs gave the little nymphs a ride on their backs. Dymion, Mark thought, seemed soberer today—almost chastened; and Rosina looked almost happy.

The weather was still coolish, and in this varied and friendly company the trip into the forest was quite pleasant. Mark fingered his laser, but Lucius said, "The Mother has driven all dangerous beasts away from her presence." And Xathax nodded in solemn agreement.

"What's happened to Kim and Helen?" asked Meriam.

Lucius looked at her with a curious smile. "Perhaps we shall see," he replied.

Then they were at the clearing.

Once more the place was light and still. In the broad path or avenue beyond, they saw a few green fauns hesitating. These now disappeared into the trees on either side, and the Plant was left to the newcomers.

Lucius acted as master of ceremonies—almost as High Priest. "Wait here," he whispered to the others, and went up to the Plant.

"Mark!" breathed Meriam, gripping his arm, "what's happened? It's different."

Two of the great boat-petals, ninety degrees apart around the radial body of the Plant, had swelled to enormous size—they were now globes as big as the central sphere. But whereas the central sphere was dark pink and opaque, these excrescent globes were glassy, covered with shimmering and moving veins of several colors like the film of a soap bubble. They were half transparent, too.

Inside each lay a bulky body, a dim tangle of limbs moving very slightly as though afloat on a liquid.

Suddenly Mark guessed. He whispered to Meriam:

"There are two in there—people, or things. Being processed. I suppose we must have looked like that, from the outside, when we thought we were merely having a dream."

Lucius was not looking at the shimmering globes. He stepped forward slowly, ceremoniously, and plucked one of the cakes from the end of a leaf-bearing arm, and carefully ate it.

Dymion said quietly: "My father is now entering fully into this Mind. I can half feel it myself."

Then, as Lucius stepped back a pace or two, the lips of the central sphere began to vibrate: Mmmmmmmm . . .

"She's going to hypnotize us again," said Meriam. She shook her head stubbornly. "I don't like that. I won't—"

But then the humming stopped. And suddenly, the shimmering transparent spheres became crystal-clear above, and burst like bubbles. The whole top of each sphere shriveled, rolled downward, turning back into a boat-shaped petal. The bodies within were disclosed, drained of liquid, stranded.

"What?" said Meriam. "Why, they're centaurs!"

Mark stared at the two sleeping creatures, wondering what was wrong with their shapes and textures. They seemed almost raw, unfledged, and shortened front to back. Then he realized. They were not formed quite like Xathax and Xilifil. They did have the basic centaur body plan, with equine tail, humanoid front feet and digitigrade, tiptoed rear feet; but they were smaller than the adult centaurs Mark knew, their rear bodies shorter, their fronts no taller than Mark himself. Their skins were bare and colored a deep golden brown; their tails and humanoid head hair were black. Their ears and facial features were perfectly human, and their feet five-toed, their hands five-fingered. They had human pubic hair and genitals between their front legs; and the girl-centaur had beautifully shaped golden-brown breasts and brown nipples. She—she was strikingly good-looking in her strange way, and somehow familiar; she reminded him of Helen. . . .

Then the girl-centaur stretched, yawned, blinked. From the way she moved, the way she turned her head, Mark, with a numbing shock, was suddenly sure that she *was* Helen—a Helen with dark-brown eyes, black hair, and four legs!

The boy centaur was coming awake now too, and he was—or had been—Kim Lee.

Mark was speechless. Meriam invoked the name of the Lord. Dymion said: "Well, Kim's done it at last. The little beast! Incarnate and imbrute . . . installed in a stallion. And Helen, my frolic filly, you may now stand four square—"

"Oh, shut up," said Rosina furiously. "Is this a time to be facetious? They're maimed, monstrous—"

"On the contrary," said Dymion, "I think they're fulfilled. Kim was never more than half human anyway, and Helen was always longing to run about on all fours. If their new apparatus *works,* then they should both be quite happy. Ah, look now!"

The new centaurs were scrambling to their feet. The apparatus did work: they were standing up.

And Mark, with his new Dextran faculty of empathy, was standing up with them, four-footed, on the drained petals. With a strange joy he discerned the movements and tensions of strange bones and muscles, the forward and backward pelvis, the double sets of ribs, the tiptoed rear toepads, the tails . . . and knew, dimly, the unique interior sensation of sex organs so far separated from the excretory system. . . .

Helen looked round her, bewildered, and passed her

hands over her naked brown flanks and withers, and flexed her rear toes.

"O my gods!" she said. "So it wasn't just a dream!"

She gave a bound, and was out of the petal, meeting her mate Kim, clasping him hand to hand, touching breasts—and laughing.

Xathax stepped forward a pace, and said gravely, "Hail, andro-centaurs! May your new tribe increase. So greet you the Wise Serpents, who will find you pasturelands, woods and glades alongside our marches. You will be wilder ones than ourselves, I perceive; but let us nevertheless be friends and neighbors, in the amity of the Mother."

"It's perfect—perfect," said Helen, surveying herself and Kim all over. "Dear, dear Hexate! She knew exactly what we wanted. My feet—they'll never hurt now, I won't tire under this gravity, I won't burn, and—"

"And you are also true natives," said Lucius, "of the *right* flesh. Here: eat of these." And he handed to Helen and Kim a couple of the Plant-cakes.

They ate: and an expression of awe came upon both their faces. They were silent for a minute or so, standing rapt, looking toward the Plant. Mark thought Helen had never been so beautiful, so full of animal grace. He did not lust after her now, but he experienced the enormous force of her own longing for the wilderness. The feelings came through, but not the thoughts, the silent speech.

At last the two new centaurs relaxed, and Helen said, "So—we're *fertile* in this form! Our tribe *will* increase. Kim, my love: shall we go for a run?"

And without more words the two bounded off, and disappeared out of the clearing into the dark forest.

"There go your true Adam and Eve of this planet," said Dymion. "Right human centaurs, and not a bit reluctant in their Paradise. The centaur form—that's the ultimate adaptation, of course—Helen and Kim were right to choose it: their children will be nice *stable* folk, not like us totterers. But I suppose some of us have our prejudices. How about you two? Do you still want to renounce your naturalization?"

Mark looked at Meriam: they both nodded.

"I'm not Helen," said Meriam, "and Mark's not Kim."

"Then," said Lucius tautly, "you had better eat, and speak, and let Wisdom speak to you."

He gave them each a cake. They pressed each other's hands, and ate.

That cake must have been a powerful drug, he thought. His head seemed to be expanding, exploding. . . . A humming filled the whole world. He was aware of many minds, a whole network: Meriam close to him, and a little farther off Lucius, farther still the minds of Helen and Kim, and of innumerable Dextran creatures of greater or lesser intellectual power. "Farther" and "closer" were ways of thinking of it: but these were degrees of vividness, of rapport, not of physical distance, or not of that alone. Pervading everything was one strong pattern of thought, with a local focus, a murmur emerging from that humming—She. The Mother. And the murmur now crystallized into something like English words.

—Lo you there, movers, little ones, it said. Greetings and blessings. We have longed to bless you thus for many revolutions, but you would not . . .

Who are *you?* said Mark, in the same form of mental speech.

—You have called us Hexate, some of you. In ourselves we have no names—you are the givers of names. Call us Hexate if you will; but that name comes with some fear. Call us, if you like, Dextra.

Why do you say *we?* inquired Mark. Is there not *one* of you here.

—There is one closest. But there are many flowerings

over the warm wet lands. If you speak with this close one, you speak with all.

Tell us, said Mark, why you have done this to us. Why have you transformed our chemistry?

—So that you may be happy. So that you may eat of our fruits. So that we may speak together.

Then if we are of Earthly substance, we cannot speak —like this?

—That is so. The two directions of Life are not equally favored. The direction you call *right-handed* has the advantage in communication. You yourself see now how it is: when a focus reaches the level of clear intellect, among us it is not altogether enclosed. It is aware of Other. With the left-handed direction, it is not so. Most left foci are quite unaware of their sibs, and even the most gifted of them are feeble in this kind of speech. Only one strain of you in five hundred revolutions have we been able to contact at all, that strain you call the Lee, and even that but dimly. It was so even with the best recent focus, Lucius, until he came to us, and was translated.

Why are the two sorts of life so different? asked Mark.

—There can be no answer to that question, not even in mind-words: for all word-answers are inside the universe, and to resolve that question one would have to move outside the universe. But we believe the difference is of the nature of existence itself. As there can be no *up* without *down,* so our dexterity implies earthly gaucheness. If that difference were dissolved, surely the universe itself would cease to be.

Tell us about yourselves, said Mark. How did you reach this level of organization? What is your relation to the fauns? And the centaurs? And what was your purpose in sending out your fauns across the sea?

—We will explain, said Hexate-Dextra.

And so Mark learned the whole astounding story.

The Plants, largest of the octofungoids, were the first Dextran life forms to become highly intelligent. Through millions of years they had flourished in New Asia. At first they were pure carnivores. They had learned various methods of attracting insects to the central mouth—sound waves, perfumes. Larger animals had been lured to lie down in the baths of the boat-petals, and there enveloped —and digested.

(—But with the bigger animals this was painful to us, said Hexate. We felt their pain.)

The Plants had begun to develop, consciously, a different mode of nutrition—photosynthesis. Four of the eight arms had been modified as leafbearers. The males of the Plants (which were much smaller, and less intelligent) now subsisted entirely on their cyanophyll, their "boat-organs" being reduced to pollinators. The females, the Plants proper, had not been able to go that far; but they had given up eating higher animals.

On the other hand, there had been animals that preyed on the Plants. The Plants could uproot themselves and move away to safer places, but only slowly. For emergencies they had developed various defenses, including mental ones.

They also entered into a symbiotic relationship with a certain bat-monkey. This monkey was fed with the Plants' cakes, and in return helped to drive off predators and to spread spores. As the Plants' mental defenses became more powerful, the relationship became more one-sided, till finally the monkeys were little more than pets. They lost their wings; they became the earliest gobblers.

The Plants, full of goodwill to all high forms of life, sought means to improve their little friends. With their long-matured chemical skills, they developed their own organs, changing the carnivorous petal-baths into chambers for mammal metamorphosis and genetic engineering. They gave the gobblers greater strength, size and longevity, and removed their vestigial midlimb skeleton. Later, when developments quickened, they removed their tails.

—As we have done to you, said Hexate.

What? said Mark and Meriam, in mental chorus.

—Yes, certain bones in your tail ends are unnecessary to humans. We have simplified your structure there, when you last came to this flowering. Also we removed your appendixes, and certain surface blemishes.

—We are full of goodwill to Earth humans, only sad that they have partly spoiled this world. We wish them to stop spoiling. There is no need for them to destroy right-handed life: if they come to us, we will translate them all, and then they will be able to share this planet with us in friendship and communion. As we share it with the native centaurs, another species that has made contact with us lately.

—As regards the little ones you now call fauns, we have been altering them more rapidly for the last two hundred revolutions, and most rapidly within the last revolution as our skill grew with practice. We did this because we hoped they might be our envoys to Earthmen. They were not fully intelligent at first, and it took us some time to discover how to improve their intelligence. We did so. We also made their form more human, for two reasons, the first being instrumental to the second. First, we perceive that humans are strangely concerned with matters of surface form—they like better a creature that is like them in structure and appearance. We hope the last version of the faun will meet with men's fullest approval.

—Our second reason was this: we wish to make ourselves more available to men. Our spores cannot survive desiccation, nor much exposure to salt sea air, and we ourselves do not flourish in great cold or dryness. Thus till now we have not been able to spread around the north of the gulf you call Euxin, nor across the Midbar Desert, nor across the sea. But the fauns are now helping us to enter the land of New Europe; they have carried our spores in their thick head hair on the last voyage. Above all, we have been hoping that suitably disposed humans might come here, impelled by curiosity about the origin of the fauns—humans who will *agree to carry spores* where fauns cannot go, namely into the land of Livya, the main seat of human power. Humans such as yourselves, Mark-Meriam.

Impossible! cried Meriam. No, no, we won't do it. Would you have us be traitors to our own people; Hexate?

—We wish your people nothing but good. If we are available, growing in the moister parts of Livya—for we believe your people have improved the climate there of late, and there are some moist parts—then we shall be able to translate the entire people of Livya, and the Saints will no longer need to hurt this world.

It couldn't be done, protested Mark. They have inspectors in Livya—they go around eradicating purple vegetation. You couldn't possibly grow there unnoticed.

—We think we could. With your cooperation. We are aware of the problems, but they can be solved. We can feed you two from our own substance, on certain concentrated foods which need only water . . . until a Flowering is established in Livya; then you will bring people to it, by ones and twos, until the whole of them are translated, converted.

Lucius broke into the mental conversation: —You should do exactly what the Mother says. It is the best consummation that could be wished for the human race on this world—on any world.

Mark pondered. It certainly seemed in some ways an attractive proposition, if it could be managed. This Dextran mind-mingling was blissful! If mankind had *that,* perhaps every age-old problem would be solved. Those wretched Saints with their holy knives would be swept away—no more Scars, on a man's flesh or on the surface of the planet. No more poisoned seas. No more misunderstandings between man and man, or man and woman . . .

Mark, said Meriam. All that is true: but we wouldn't be human.

Lucius produced the mental equivalent of a sneer: —Human! All too human! It is time we gave up being that. A wretched, barbarous race, cut off from all true mental contact, and proud of its limitations.

Limitations, said Meriam, yes. Even our limitations have a right to exist.

—We will abide by your decision, said Dextra-Hexate. We have learned by the history of the fauns; we no longer wish to manage other high life forms without their own consent. If we come to you, we will leave you free will. And now, what do you say?

I say no, said Meriam. I bear you no ill will, Dextra, and I hope you will continue to flourish in your own native lands. But Livya is now an *Earthly* land, full of Earthly people. Whatever their faults, I will not help to make them unEarthly. And—although I shall miss this contact of minds—I wish to be translated back again, if you can manage that. I want to return to my own limited *human* life.

There was a great humming silence. Finally the words came:

—And Mark. You? Will you be our envoy?

Yes, said Mark, Hexate-Dextra, I will—

Meriam uttered a mental cry of anguish. O Mark, Mark, will you be lost to me—

—but, continued Mark, Dextra, I will be your envoy only openly, as a man goes openly to other men who are his friends. I will not carry spores by stealth, or help to take over Livya for you. There are better ways, I think, of achieving friendship between you and men. And, Dextra, if you can do what Meriam has asked—translate us back to our limited, left-handed life—then I want that for myself also.

Fools! shouted Lucius mentally. Blind, blind selfish fools, traitors to the best hope—

—Let us now keep silence, said the humming voice. We need to meditate.

The humming grew louder. It was almost intolerable. Meriam huddled, physically, against Mark: they clasped each other. Then the sounds died into murmurs.

—We have decided. Mark-Meriam, you have spoken not unwisely. We shall work for friendship with men slowly, gradually. Already there are planted spores beyond the fences of Sunion: sooner or later there will be many Flowerings in New Europe, and many men who come to them and choose to be translated. Even some who will wish for a more efficient shape, like Helen-Kimon. In another hundred revolutions, there will be many intelligent species of movers in this world, most of them of right-handed substance; and then the right-handed ones will no longer need to fear those of the left.

—Also we wish to express some gratitude to Man, even limited, fearful, destructive Man, our invader. Before the coming of Man, there were no words in the minds of Dextra. You strange little movers—through the medium of the Lee strain—you have given us words, and through words quicker, keener thought. We could not have accomplished what we have recently accomplished without you—the transformations of the fauns, and latterly of yourselves. Thus, our coming together has been fertile for us both.

—But now, for many revolutions, we must hide ourselves away from this coast, and conceal our doings with the fauns, so as to avoid too abrupt a contact with the Livyans. We know you will aid us in this, Mark-Meriam . . . and in return we will do to you that which you have desired—if you still desire it.

We do, said Mark and Meriam at once.

—An exact reversal? said the humming voice. Defects as well?

Please, said Mark and Meriam. Only—you may omit to restore the Scar.

—The embryo, said the voice. That will have to be translated also.

What! cried Meriam, what embryo?

—You are not aware? Little mover Meriam, since we translated you, you have been fertilized. Your spore is half a day old. It has been right-handed since its first moment, but if you are translated now, so must your spore be, or it will die. We will have to limit its life to the left-hand path.

My baby, cried Meriam. Will it be hurt by what you do?

—Not in the least, except in the usual human limitation. It will grow into a normal one of your male variety. The operation at this stage is of the simplest . . .

Meriam, now gripped tightly by Mark, bowed her head: —O my son, forgive me: I must be what I must be, merely human; and so therefore must you.

—If you are ready, said the Plant, then lay yourselves naked in the nearest petal. One petal will suffice.

The humming faded. Mark and Meriam became aware of the physical world to a much greater extent. The others were helping them: Rosina was undressing Meriam, Dymion and Xathax were pulling off Mark's clothes.

They lay down together in the petal, and saw the iridescent edges curling upward, cutting them off from the outside world.

Faint humming words came to them in their secret bed:

—Mark-Meriam, fare you well. You will not hear this voice again. When next we speak, it will be to your bodies. Blessings, little movers, and farewell. . . .

"Oh Mark," cried Meriam, aloud, embracing him, "goodbye!"

"Don't be afraid, dear—"

"I'm not afraid. But dear, when we wake, we won't be *in* each other any more. I'll just be me—you'll just be you. I shall miss being partly you."

"And I you," he said sleepily, "my lover, my love . . ."

Love enveloped them in warm streams. As once before, Mark felt himself being taken, all his secret places probed by infinitesimal fingers. His beloved put her hand in at the holes, and his bowels were moved at her touch . . . but, but, this time there was no ecstasy, only a soul-tearing sensation of loss. . . .

. . . As before, Meriam felt herself being taken, and her bowels were moved at that touch. She opened to her beloved . . . but, but, her beloved had withdrawn himself, and was gone, and her soul failed . . . she called him, but he gave no answer. A soul-tearing sensation of loss. . . .

He woke into a hard, clear world. He was only a man. There were people standing about. Beside him in the dry petal there was a naked girl. He ended at his own skin, and knew nothing of the Other, beyond.

He nearly screamed.

But then the girl beside him took him by the shoulders, and he felt her tears falling on his skin.

"Mark," said Meriam, managing a little smile, "Mark, we're back."

When they clambered out of the petal, they saw Lucius sitting on the ground, his head bowed, apparently drained of energy. Rosina, Dymion and the centaurs seemed simply glad to see them. The little faun-maids sadly, wordlessly handed them their clothes.

They had hardly finished dressing when Lucius uttered a cry.

"The Mother! You have rejected her—and now she is leaving us!"

Xathax placed his strong hand on the old man's shoulder.

"Calmly, old friend. She is merely performing that which she so wisely decreed."

They had all turned, and were gazing at the Plant—which now began to reveal its true nature as, after all, a strange type of animal.

With almost infinite slowness, but visibly, the central sphere was rising out of the ground. Mark watched the process, spellbound. After several minutes, the sphere stood clear, supported by many dozens of rootletlike legs on the floor of the hollow it had once dug for itself. Then, much more quickly, the petals and leaf-bearing arms rolled back, folding in on top of the sphere till the whole creature was a compact mass taller than it was wide. Finally, it began to creep away, very ponderously at first out of its hollow, then rather faster across the clearing until it had gained the broad avenue beyond. As it retreated along this, Mark heard the soft burbling of fauns in the trees on either side of the avenue. The sound grew fainter. The forest children were escorting their Mother.

It was a sober march that they now made, Mark, Meriam and their companions, back through the forest. At the river, Xathax and Xilifil said goodbye.

"We must go catch those wild ones, Kim and Helen," said Xathax, "and take care of them. Then the Wise Serpents will be moving farther inland. Along with much else."

"Along with me," said Lucius grimly. "I have no further need of my books, nor any more contact with humans. I resign the stead to you, Dymion. I will follow the Mother."

Dymion explained: "While you two were being—er—processed, Father got his instructions. The golden super-fauns are going to disappear from these parts along with the centaurs, native and human—because it seems the government of Livya—I mean GenCon—they're going to take an interest in Anthis. *We* may have to move, ourselves—I don't know."

When Lucius and the centaurs had gone, Meriam looked sadly at the faithful nymphs, Circe and Chloe.

"Aren't you going to leave us too?" she said.

"Oh, no, Mistress," said Chloe brightly. "We have had our orders also. We are to stay, and be caught."

"Caught?" said Mark.

"By the men who will come," said Circe. "At least, some of us will be caught. Mayhap we and some others may stay with Maister Dymion."

"Not too many, I hope," said Rosina under her breath.

"By the way," said Mark to Rosina and Dymion, "what happened to you? Didn't Lucius offer you the great translation too?" He stared at them. "Did you by any chance—while we were in there—"

"Most certainly not," said Rosina. "I have always felt like Meriam about this—I have no wish to be cut off from the human race, from my children. And Dymion has his own reasons, too."

Dymion laughed. "It wouldn't do for me, Mark. I have quite enough witchcraft for my purposes already. I couldn't use the mystical vision and all that as well." He paused. "The fact is, not only the fauns, but also the centaurs—they don't write poetry. They're too contented, too integrated. I'd rather keep my limitations—and go on writing my pieces. They're poor things, but mine own."

When they reached Flora, it was a hot bright afternoon. There were a few faun servants about, and some came running to meet them on the meadow called Concord where the green and blue grass grew mingled. They were pointing toward the river.

Their explanations were drowned by a shattering, mechanical roar.

It was a few moments before Mark could place that alien sound. Then he said, "Why—surely—that's a skimmer!"

It was. They found the skimmer tying up next to the *Naiad,* directly in front of the house.

"Why," said Meriam, "I do believe it's that Navy boat—the one that took us to Sunion. I wonder what they can be doing here?"

The black-jackets were swarming onto the landing dock, and now Captain Heber marched forward. He smiled, and extended his left hand to Mark. Mark took it, almost awkwardly. Then Heber shook Meriam's left hand also, and said, "We called in at Sunion a couple of days back, and interviewed the family there. We saw and heard certain things, and we consulted by radio with the Holy City—and we are here on a mission." He looked at Dymion, in his cloak and loincloth, with distinct distaste. "You the steader here? Master Lee, isn't it?"

"Yes," said Dymion. "I am the steader here, now."

"Well, we've been ordered to clear you out. No settlement on this coast has ever been authorized, you have no official holding, and now it seems there are intelligent native life forms—yes, here they are," he said, looking at the green fauns and nymphs. "I reported to GenCon what I saw at Sunion, and I must say, you seem to be running a regular slave trade. This has got to stop."

Dymion raised his eyebrows. "Since when is GenCon run by purple-lovers?"

Heber looked evasive. "Well, there are different schools of thought, you know. I'm a Moderate, myself—a Two-Gardenite. The Total Eradicators were beaten on the last vote. And so, Master Lee, I'm happy to say your precious little racket in cahoots with the Anders family is now at an end."

"Fair enough," said Dymion, shrugging. "I was pressured into it, anyway. But why do we have to leave Flora?"

"I've told you—no authorization. Besides, GenCon doesn't want settlers on this coast if there are intelligent natives here. Settlers might foul up our relations with them. Above all, we want to investigate them first, see what species there are, before we decide whether to plant colonies in New Asia. Master Turner, you're a zoologist —what have you discovered about these little green folk?"

Mark shrugged. "Only that they're a species akin to the common gobbler and the blueskins. The blueskins and these greenskins are certainly rational, but there are not all that many of them. They don't pose any kind of threat to humans."

"Good, good. Well, I hope you two had a good vacation." Heber turned back to Dymion. "Master Lee, I'm going to leave a couple of my men with you, to help you evacuate your stead. The men'll help you sail that tub of yours back to Classica—and make sure you go there. Got any other family?"

"No," said Dymion, "not any more. My father—well, he passed on. He wasn't young, you know."

Heber accepted a clipboard from one of his men. "Weren't there a couple of young people?" he said, glancing at his papers. "I checked at Sunion—"

"You do keep tabs on us, don't you?" said Dymion. "Yes, my brother and his girl. Sorry about them. A sad accident in the jungle—wild beasts. Nothing left of them, I'm afraid."

Heber looked grave. "This really dosen't seem a good place for human settlement. Too dangerous by half! I shall report accordingly. Best leave it to these greenies."

"Oh," said Dymion, "we shall take a few of them with us. Not as slaves—they want to visit their friends in Classica. Circe and Chloe do, anyway."

"We shall check that you treat them right," said Heber. "My men will be looking after them during your voyage."

"Thank Heaven for that," said Rosina.

Dymion laughed. "Oh, Rosy, I shall reform this time—really I will. We'll set up stead somewhere in Classica, and get back the kids from my mother, and—watch certain plants grow."

Mark and Meriam had been standing apart, holding hands, and chatting with the two little nymphs. Meriam whispered to Circe, "May your twins be fine healthy handsome little fauns!"

"Oh," said Circe brightly, "they are sure to be that, Mistress. The Mother always brings them out perfect. May she bless your little boy even so."

Heber now turned to Mark and Meriam.

"What about you two? Shall I give you a lift back to Sunion? I can—but otherwise my course would be straight back to Livya."

"That'll suit us fine," said Mark. "We've had a very full field trip already. Now we feel like getting down to some work—absorbing our results, faking up some stuff to show our supervisors—you know how it is."

"And," said Meriam, "we've got some academic correspondence to attend to—we have to write to some people in Atlantis."

"Sure, sure," said Heber, nodding sagely. "All that paperwork. I have enough of it, myself."

"Oh yes, and there's another thing we have to do, just as soon as we get back," said Mark. "Our families will be expecting it, and we don't want to disappoint them, and frankly we would be in trouble now if we didn't do it."

"What's that?" said Heber.

Meriam laughed. "Get married," she said.

APPENDIX I:

Map of Dextra

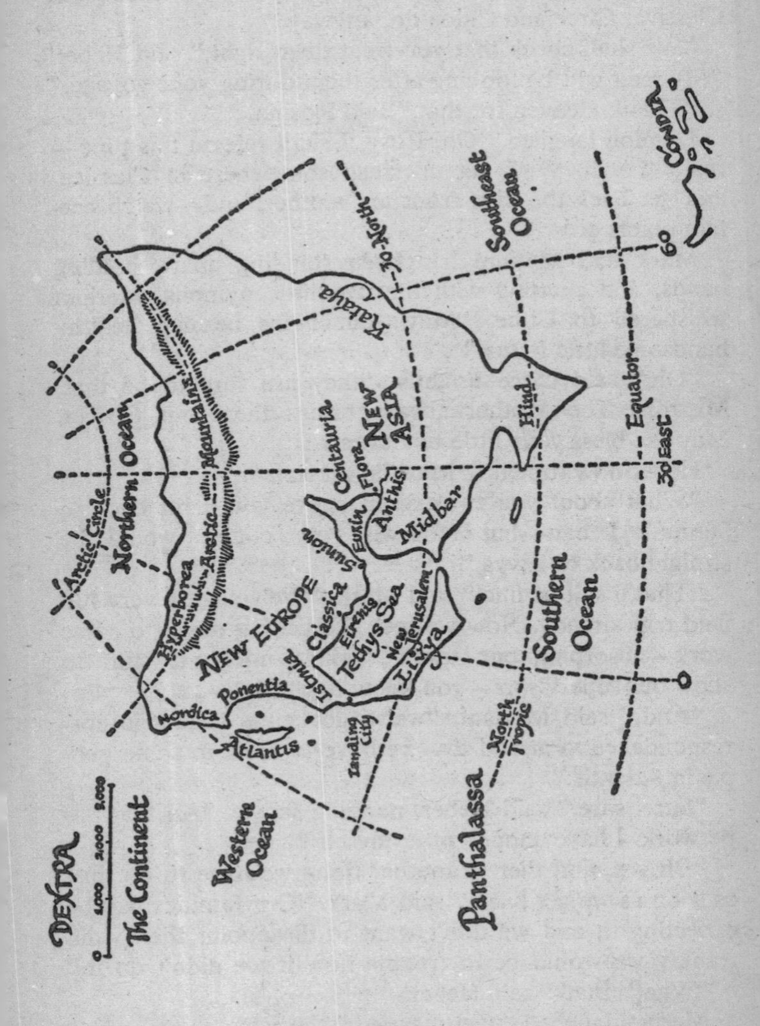

Appendix II: Full text of "The Centaur"

(Authorship doubtful: Endymion Lee? Andrew Marvell?)

The Centaur

Harmonious Monster, whose strange Shape
Commits on Kind most pleasant rape,
Both Man and Beast may envy thee
Thy four-footed dexterity.
This Steed his eyes to Heav'n may raise
And take his meat with hands, not grace:
This Man forgets not to be wise
In the Earth's deep humilities,
And planted firm, fears not at all
To stumble, or like *Adam* fall;
So well may he be call'd alone
Of Animals the Paragon;
Apotheosis of the Horse,
Matchless to run, stand or discourse.
Alas, for Fancy! this bright *Plan*
Of better Horse, of stabler Man,
Our Stepdame World of duller Earth
Could not conceive, or bring to birth.
This wanted Link in the great Chain
Was forged in some Poet's brain,
And god-like sprung in days of old
Into that *Thessaly* of gold,
Of Faun and Nymph and Hero-youth,
That never was in sober sooth.
Plato play'd false, accusing Art
To mock the Life: the better part
Is Poesy's, not to imitate
This Earth of lead, but new create
Far other Worlds, transcending this

As much as Heav'n does earthly bliss,
And Paradises of the Mind
Where we may such sweet Creatures find
As (pricking on some Heav'nly Plain)
This Horseman of the human Brain.